THE SHADOW OF THE UNICORN: THE LEGACY

SUZANNE DE MONTIGNY

MuseItYoung, division of
MuseItUp Publishing
www.museituppublishing.com

MuseItUp Publishing
14878 James, Pierrefonds, Quebec, Canada, H9H 1P5

Cover Art © 2012 by Marion Sipe
Edited by Lea Schizas
Layout and Book Production by Lea Schizas

Print ISBN: 978-1-77127-615-3
eBook ISBN: 978-1-77127-225-4
Production by MuseItUp Publishing

Remember the rhinos and elephants in Africa
who are threatened with extinction.

Acknowledgements

A huge thank you to my writer's groups, particularly Kathi Sprayberry for her extraordinary patience over the past five years. To my wonderful editor, Lea Schizas, for all her help getting my story in shape. To my mom for the small unicorn that stands on my table reminding me she believes in me no matter what.

And the biggest thanks of all to the three loves of my life—my husband who allowed me to stay home and write, and my two wonderful boys who were the first to love my story.

Author's Note: 20% of all proceeds will go to the Third World Eye Care Society, a group of eye specialists who travel to third world countries delivering thousands of pairs of glasses, and performing eye surgery for free.

Chapter One

The Valley

Azaria strained his skinny legs and pushed his way up the mountain. His white fur glistened with sweat and he puffed hard, drawing in as much air as he could. His father, Polaris, led the way. The unicorn colt admired his father's strong muscles, and the long, spiraled ivory horn that crowned his head. He wished he could climb the slope as easily as his father, breathing normally like he was on flat land, instead of groaning and gasping for air.

"Let's stop for a rest," said Polaris.

"All right, if *you* need to," said Azaria, his legs trembling. "I don't really need a break. I'm perfectly fine." The colt collapsed onto his haunches and gulped for more air. He caught a glimpse of a smile when his father turned his head. "What's so funny?" he asked, leaning his head to one side.

"Oh, nothing," said Polaris, straightening his mouth.

The two unicorns rested in the shade of the tall mountain trees. Bird songs echoed in the forest. The aroma of the ferns tickled Azaria's nose, and he sneezed hard between heavy breaths.

"Bless you," said Polaris.

The colt sneezed again.

"Bless you again." He laughed.

Polaris turned to gaze at the snow-covered peaks and the valley below.

Azaria followed his father's eyes, and then asked the question that burned inside him. "So why did you bring me here, Father? Just to see the view?"

His father chuckled, and then grew serious. "No. It's because we've been summoned."

"Summoned?" Azaria said, fanning himself with his tail.

"Yes," said Polaris.

"You mean by that thing that scared the mares this morning?" His heart raced at the memory of the strange, little animal that dashed into the herd, wheezing. About the size of a fox, it looked like no other lizard he'd ever seen with its sharp teeth, claws, and even feathers.

"I wasn't scared at all," Azaria babbled between breaths. "After all, it was just a funny looking lizard...right?" He tilted his head and looked at Polaris, hopeful.

Polaris grinned. "No. He was a messenger—from the dinosaurs."

"The dinosaurs?" The colt's eyes grew wide. "You mean like the Rexus?"

Azaria had heard stories about these giant, flesh-eating dinosaurs that shook the ground as they walked, their long tails sweeping behind. One of them even devoured a unicorn many years before he was born.

"No, not the Rexus." Polaris shook his head. "Saul, the Great Chief. He's asked that we leave tomorrow. He says it's urgent. Apparently, there are strange things going on over there."

"What's been happening?" The colt frowned.

"I don't know yet, but I'm taking *you* with me."

"What?" Azaria pricked his ears forward.

"I'm taking *you* with me." Polaris repeated himself. "You're six moons old now, and you need to know as much as you can about our valley and what lies beyond."

Azaria's eyes bulged. "But why me?"

"Because you may be leader someday." Polaris smiled.

"Me? Leader of the unicorns?"

"Yes." He nodded.

Azaria looked far below at the white unicorns gathered in the valley. Tingles ran down his spine at the thought of becoming the Great Stallion.

"Look at how many there are—hundreds of us," said Polaris, his voice filled with pride.

Azaria squinted at the creatures glistening on the plain, white specks dotting the lush, green banks of the river.

"There's no other creature as striking as the unicorn." Polaris pointed to the sunrise end of the valley with his horn. "That's Zeus' herd over there," he said, then turned to where the sun set. "And that's Solomon's."

"There are three herds?" asked Azaria.

Polaris nodded, and then pointed toward the distant mountains. "And you see that tall mountain?"

"Yeah."

"That's where the dinosaurs dwell. And that's where we're going tomorrow."

Azaria stretched his neck. Spying the snow-capped peak in the far distance, he cried, "I see it!" His tail twitched back and forth as visions of magnificent beasts filled his head. Then fear gripped him. "Father, what if we get eaten by a Rexus?"

"Don't worry. We'll stay as far away from them as we can. The valley's wide, and they only occupy certain areas."

The colt heaved a sigh of relief, and then furrowed his brows. "Father, why do the Rexus eat other dinosaurs—and unicorns?"

"That's just how it is. They eat meat. Just like the lions eat zebra." He lowered his head and broke off a mouthful of grass.

Azaria shuddered. "Zebras? Gross! That's like eating dead unicorns."

"Mm-hm." Polaris chewed.

Azaria continued. "Okay, but if the lions like zebra, then wouldn't they like unicorn meat too?"

The stallion swallowed his mouthful of grass, and then answered, "No. They're afraid of us. They learned long ago a lion is no match for a unicorn. If they attack us, we can kill them with the tip of our horns."

"So we're enemies?"

"No. It's more like we don't bother them and they don't bother us."

"Then only the Rexus are our enemies?" Azaria asked.

"That's right." Polaris rose from his resting spot and shook his coat.

"Then why do the dinosaurs live in the other valley?"

"Because there's not enough food for us all. We chose to live apart long ago." He took a few steps forward, heading down the path. "The sun's getting low. It's time we joined the herd. Your mother's waiting."

Azaria scrambled up, his legs still shaky from the climb. They descended into the valley, picking their way down the steep slopes. The herd grazed peacefully in the late afternoon sun.

He loved this part of the valley where they lived. The grass was tender here, with sweet purple flowers that grew between the tall, green blades. Close by, a small brook meandered to the river. And near the creek, stood the large banyan tree where they all met and cooled themselves on hot days, and gathered to sleep at night.

Azaria hurried past the two fillies, Cassi and Jemmi.

"Azaria, come on," they called, giggling as he ran past like they usually did.

"Not now," he said, picking up speed despite his tired legs. He spied his mother, Aurora, nearby. "Mother, have you seen Gaelan?"

Aurora raised her head, eyes shining as she gazed at her son. "No, but you're a clever colt. You'll find him. Just look around."

Not always clever.

He remembered the sharp nip on his rump he'd earned after an ill-fated plan the other day.

Then it came—Azaria heard the loud neigh he was waiting for.

"Looking for me?" Gaelan came bounding up to his friend. "What happened? What did you see?" He cantered in circles around Azaria, nearly tripping over his own hooves. Azaria tried not to laugh. It wasn't Gaelan's fault he had such long legs that made him clumsy.

He told Gaelan about his day on the mountain.

"So that was a dinosaur this morning? Whoa!" Gaelan bounced as he chattered. "And he says something strange has been going on?"

"Yeah," Azaria said, "Father says we're going tomorrow."

"Wow! Really? Hey, you think he might take me to see them too?"

"You never know. I could ask him."

"Yeah!" Gaelan kicked his back hooves out. "Hey, let's play dinosaurs and unicorns. I'll be the Rexus, and you can be the unicorn."

"But I don't want to be eaten." Azaria scowled. "Unless I can kill you first."

"But I don't want to be killed."

"Okay, you can eat me first, and then I can kill you," said Azaria.

"Okay."

The two colts played together until the shadows grew long and their eyes heavy. The sun set boldly that night. Bright oranges and golds filled the sky. Azaria curled up close to his dam under the Banyan tree. He just couldn't wait until the next day. But for now, he needed to sleep.

Chapter Two

The Dinosaurs

The rising sun stretched its golden tendrils across the earth, warming the cool land, when Polaris whispered to a sleeping Azaria the next morning, "Wake up. We're going to see the dinosaurs."

Azaria grumbled and turned over, and then jerked his head up, struggling to his feet. "Really, Father? Are we really?" he asked, his voice croaky like the toads he heard calling at night.

"Yes, if you can wake up." Polaris grinned.

"Can we take Gaelan?" Azaria asked, shaking the dew off his coat.

"Sure. After all, he may be a leader someday too. It's important for you both to learn how to speak to these creatures. Let's go get him."

Father and colt crept quietly to where the other young unicorn slept, curled beneath his dam's hooves.

"Gaelan," whispered Azaria as loud as he could, nearly hissing with excitement, "we're going to the dinosaur's valley!" The colt didn't stir. Azaria nudged his friend with his nose and whispered louder, "Gaelan, we're going to see the dinosaurs!"

The slumbering colt shot up, stumbling sideways. Shaking his mane and snorting, he turned to his dam, his eyes pleading, "Can I please, Mother?"

Elissa nodded and the two colts bounded after Polaris, prancing and nickering softly so as not to wake the other foals.

The sun had journeyed a little higher over the horizon, painting the sky a gentle rose hue and awakening the colors throughout the valley. Warm steam escaped from the unicorns' nostrils. Azaria shivered, but dared not complain in case his father decided he was too young for the long trek. As the sun rose higher into the sky, its comforting warmth felt good on his back. After a while, he began to observe changes along the way.

"Gaelan, have you noticed there are a lot more ferns here? And look, pine trees," said Azaria.

"Yeah. I wonder why?" replied Gaelan, raising his head up to take it all in.

"It's dinosaur food," said Polaris. "Nothing tastier to a dinosaur... except if you're a Rexus, that is."

Azaria quivered at his father's words. "And did you notice there aren't many birds around here either? I don't even hear one singing."

"Neither do I," said Gaelan. "Weird." He shook his head.

They soon found out why when a loud shriek filled the air and a small, terrified bird fled past their heads, screeching and batting its wings.

"Wha...?" exclaimed Azaria.

Swooping down from a tall tree, a large, winged reptile pursued its tiny prey. The two colts bolted. Azaria scrambled into a bush and watched while the creature captured the bird triumphantly in his sharp claws and continued on its way. Cowering and breathing hard, he waited.

"It's okay, boys. You can come out now," called Polaris. "It's just a flying dinosaur. All it eats is birds."

"Are you sure?" Gaelan asked.

"Yes. It's not interested in you. You're both too big," said Polaris, smiling.

Azaria peeked through the bush, his eyes wide, and then crept out, his tail between his legs. Gaelan clambered about, emerging from the bushes covered in brambles and mud.

"A flying dinosaur? Is that all?" asked Azaria. "Oh...Well I wasn't scared. I just thought I saw some good leaves in that bush. They're really tasty, you know. Have you tried some?" He scanned the sky to see if the winged creature would return.

Polaris gave his son the eye, grinning. "No thanks. But keep watching."

They continued on their way. Gaelan skulked behind, his head down, avoiding Azaria's gaze.

Stifling a giggle, Azaria whispered, "It's okay, Gaelan. I was scared too."

Peeking at his friend with one eye, Gaelan said, "Thanks."

When the sun had traveled high in the sky, they rounded the corner into the new valley. Azaria caught his breath. Waterfalls cascaded over cliffs of white stone, moistening the air with its mist. Carpets of fern painted the valley a lush green, while what seemed like thousands of flowers scented the air with delicate fragrances. But more breathtaking still, was the huge herd of horned dinosaurs that grazed on the emerald grass.

Azaria stared, his mouth open. These great beasts were splendid. They were huge, magnificent, and…

"They're just like us!" he exclaimed.

"What do mean just like us?" Gaelan moved closer to his friend, keeping a wary eye on the creatures before him.

"Because look…they eat grass and travel in herds like we do, and they have dams and babies too," Azaria chattered.

"Oh yeah," cried Gaelan.

But Azaria discovered they weren't the only ones surprised. The young dinosaurs gazed at them with wide eyes, too, ducking behind their dams.

Azaria chuckled. "How can they be so frightened when they're twice our size?"

"Because they're just babies," said Polaris.

"Aw, they're so cute!" cried Gaelan.

Gingerly stepping forward, Azaria approached the young ones. They scattered from his path, making strange grunting noises. He exchanged smiles with Gaelan.

An older dinosaur with strong plates surrounding his face, and wisdom in his eyes stepped forward. The adult dinosaurs made way for the large beast.

He must be the chief.

Azaria stole behind his father.

Polaris laughed. "Now watch, boys. When you speak to a dinosaur, you must be very formal. Copy what I do." As the chief approached, the stallion bowed low. "Saul," he said, "it's been a very long time. I'm honoured to be in your presence again."

The dinosaur returned the bow, his eyes sincere. "Ah, Polaris! It *has* been many months since we have seen one another. The honour is mine. I'm glad you came so quickly after my summons."

"I knew it was important." Polaris turned, his gaze falling on the two colts. "Saul, I want to present to you my son, Azaria, and his friend, Gaelan. I'm hoping they'll be leaders one day," he said, his voice slightly deeper than usual.

The noble dinosaur bowed to the wide-eyed colts. "It is my honour to make your acquaintance, oh future leaders." He smiled. "Someday, we may negotiate great things together."

Imitating his sire, Azaria bowed. Gaelan followed, stumbling a little. They watched Polaris for more cues.

Saul veered away, gesturing his head in a forward direction. Azaria, with Gaelan in tow, stepped high after the old chief, looking grown-up as possible.

Saul's heavy legs thudded, shaking the earth as he led the unicorns through the valley. "There are many different kinds of dinosaurs, young colts," the chief said. "See the tiny ones over there? They're no larger than a jackal."

Azaria recognized the messenger, but his attention was drawn further away to another dinosaur. "Whoa, look at that one," he whispered to Gaelan. "What's that thing on its head? And get a load of the sound it makes when it calls to the others!"

"Yeah. And those ones over there have three horns. Wonder what they need three for?" asked Gaelan.

"I don't know, but it'd be kind of neat to have a couple more horns, though."

"Yeah, just think of all the damage we could do!" Gaelan snorted.

Clearing his throat, Azaria changed to a most respectful voice, "Yes, they are very impressive, Chief Saul."

Azaria's eyes wandered to where dark, ominous caves stood in the mountain. He shivered. "Honourable sir, does anything live there?" he asked, trying to keep his voice steady.

Saul stopped and faced the two colts. "No one ever goes there," he said. "And you'd be wise to stay away from them too. He lowered his voice to a murmur. "That's where the Rexus live."

They scurried past, keeping at a fast trot until they reached a grassy field at the edge of the forest where they came upon a new herd of dinosaurs.

"They're gigantic!" exclaimed Azaria.

"Yes, they are. These are the largest of all the dinosaurs, but there is something..." Saul turned to Polaris, his face transformed. "Polaris, I wonder what you would make of this?"

"What, Saul?" Polaris scrunched his brow and moved a little closer to the chief.

"We have a young dinosaur within this herd that has a strange affliction. Perhaps you have seen something like this before."

Azaria cocked his head to listen. Saul had lowered his voice.

"What sort of affliction?" asked Polaris, following Saul's lead and speaking in a quiet voice.

"Well, he tells us strange things. It's most peculiar." The chief frowned.

"May I inquire as to what?" asked Polaris.

"Well...come, and see for yourself." Saul turned and led them away.

Azaria was quick to fall in line behind the two adults. Curious to meet this most odd dinosaur, he wondered if it were sick or maybe had three legs instead of four. He had heard of a unicorn born with only three legs once.

The unicorns followed the old chief further into the forest where the tall dinosaurs seemed to reach the sky as they stood munching leaves. The old chief sought out a particularly lofty female and called her. She gently lowered her head to Saul's level. Her kind eyes drew Azaria in as he listened to her musical voice.

"Hello, Saul. What brings the most graceful unicorns to us today?"

"Maresa, this is Polaris. He wanted us to meet his son Azaria and his friend Gaelan. They may be leaders someday, you know," Saul said, a smile curving his lips.

Maresa let out a tinkling laugh. "You are most welcome here, little ones."

"Thank you," both colts answered at once.

Then Saul's eyes grew serious. "Maresa, I wonder if we could speak to your son, Darius."

Maresa hesitated, and then called him. Hearing his mother, Darius trundled over and stopped short, digging his heels into the earth. His eyes were wide with fright and his breath came in short gasps. Turning to run, he halted again and turned to gawk once more at the unicorns as though they were the strangest creatures he had ever seen. Then he moved to stand before the chief, breathing quickly. Azaria stifled a giggle.

"It's okay, Darius. They're just unicorns. They live in the next valley," Saul said.

The little dinosaur stood as though baffled, staring up and down at the three. "So it's happening? The world's going to change now?" He gulped.

Azaria frowned at his mysterious words.

"What do you mean, Darius?" asked Polaris.

Darius' eyes grew distant. "I keep dreaming that the world is different," he said.

Maresa spoke up. "He gets this look in his eyes, and then he's gone. We can't talk to him because he doesn't hear us. And when he comes to, he tells these strange tales."

"What sort of tales?"

"Tell him, Darius." Maresa nudged him with her giant muzzle.

The little dinosaur sat on his haunches. "Well, there will be a cloud over everything and most of the plants will disappear," he said. "A lot of animals will die too. But there'll be new animals to replace them, creatures that walk on two legs like the Rexus. One of them, the Ishmael, will be most dangerous and everything will change."

The puzzled colts exchanged mesmerized looks.

Polaris locked eyes with Saul, but not a word passed between them. He turned back to Darius. "How will we know when all of this will begin?"

"I don't know when…just soon."

The two leaders eyed each other once more, and as though on cue, moved away to speak in private.

Saul turned to the young dinosaur. "Thank you, Darius. You may leave now. Thank you, Maresa." He nodded his head, dismissing her. Darius trundled toward the lake as though nothing unusual had happened.

"I wonder if he's a seer," whispered Azaria.

"What's a seer?" asked Gaelan.

"I heard the mares talking about them once. They have visions of things before they happen."

"Weird. Then do you really think something is about to change?" asked Gaelan.

"I don't know, but I think we better watch out for some of those things he was talking about," replied Azaria, his eyes darting about.

"Maybe he just has dreams or something," suggested Gaelan. "I know I have some really weird ones sometimes. Just last week I dreamed that my mom had grown elephant's feet."

14

Azaria laughed out loud.

He gazed at Polaris and Saul in the distance, their heads close together in conversation and wondered what they were saying. He didn't dare approach them for fear of being disrespectful. Instead, he suggested, "Let's follow Darius to the lake."

The young dinosaur had scurried away, giggling. The two colts broke into a canter and pursued him. Darius splashed his cumbersome body into the lake, the unicorns close behind. They chased him through the cool water, but were soon breathing hard.

"He might be a dinosaur, but he's pretty fast in the water," said Azaria, his legs tiring.

"Hey, where did he go?" Gaelan looked around.

Darius disappeared and resurfaced behind Gaelan. "Boo!" he shouted, laughing when Gaelan jumped.

The unicorns paddled their hooves to make their escape.

"It's no use, Gaelan, he's too fast for us." Azaria slowed down.

The three creatures stopped, all three panting like dogs, and stood in a watery circle laughing.

"You guys are fun," said Darius, catching his breath. "I'm glad we'll be able to play all the time soon."

"Well…actually…we're going home," said Gaelan.

"Yeah, but later," insisted the little dinosaur.

The two colts looked at each other, confused. Azaria wanted to explain they lived far away, but instead, chose to lie. "Yeah, soon." He caught sight of his sire in the distance. "Look, my father's leaving!"

The two leaders had strolled toward the entrance to the valley, and were bowing to one another. Azaria and Gaelan hurried to join him, careful to imitate Polaris' gestures. The sun lay low in the sky and strange night sounds crept their way into the landscape.

"Thank you, Saul. It has been a fine day and we will now be on our way," said Polaris.

"It has indeed. It has been my honour to meet these future leaders." Saul smiled warmly at the two colts. "I look forward to seeing all of you one day soon." The old dinosaur turned to leave. "Good night," he called, his huge feet thumping as he returned to the valley.

As the distance grew between the unicorns and Saul, Azaria asked, "So, how did we do? Were we serious enough?"

"You were, but we better hurry before the sun sets completely," warned Polaris. "We don't want to be anyone's supper."

"I thought you said we had no enemies," said Azaria, fear gripping him.

"That's during the day. At night, it's a whole different story. We can't see too well in the dark. We're safer in the herd," he explained.

Azaria quickened his pace. The night sounds swelled louder and louder making his hair stand on end.

Soon, the weird and wonderful noises of the dinosaurs' valley faded in the distance, and the familiar sounds of their own territory drifted in once again. Azaria was relieved to find the herd huddled together for the night under the banyan tree. Seeking out Aurora, he cuddled against her, excited to tell her of all that he had seen that day, and especially of his strange new friend Darius.

"He thinks everything will change, Mother. Do you think maybe he was a seer?"

Aurora nuzzled her colt. "I think he was having nightmares. I wouldn't worry about it. He'll soon forget about it, and everything will still be the same. You'll see," she said as Azaria's eyelids drooped, heavy with sleep. But Azaria wasn't so sure.

Chapter Three

The Meeting

"Quick! The meeting's going to start." Jemmi squealed.

Azaria pranced, pawing the air with his hooves. For days he had watched unicorn messengers travel to and fro to the various parts of the valley, announcing the gathering. He had waited far too long for this. Excited, he watched the unicorns march together in their respective herds to the spot in the middle of the valley where the river ran shallowest. There, they were met by Mohala, the eldest of all the unicorns.

"She frightens me." Cassi cowered.

"Me too," said Azaria, cringing at the aged unicorn's fierce expression.

"She has such scary eyes," said Gaelan.

"Shhh. We better listen." Azaria gulped, noting her pale blue eyes roving over the herd as though searching out anyone who dared show disrespect.

"Hail unicorns," Mohala's raspy, ancient voice rumbled, demanding their attention. "Great leaders: Solomon, Zeus, and Polaris, we have assembled here today as one great herd to hear Polaris' words."

Quieting down, the three herds pointed their horns toward the matriarch in respect. Polaris stepped forward into the center of the group.

"Unicorns, I have seen and heard something that may involve us all – something that may change our lives forever." He paused, as though heavy in thought, and then continued, "Azaria, Gaelan, and I recently traveled to the dinosaur's valley where we met Saul, their eminent leader. He introduced us to a most unusual young dinosaur named Darius, who told us some very troubling tales."

Azaria heard the soft murmur of interest as the unicorns listened.

"He speaks of a new world, one that is remarkably different from the one we inhabit today. He speaks of change, of a great cloud, of many animals dying, of disappearing plants, and most disturbing of all, a new creature that walks on two legs like the Rexus."

The unicorns mumbled.

"More monster dinosaurs?" whinnied one of the mares.

"Silence!" Mohala bellowed in her authoritative voice.

The neighs and whinnies faded. Azaria and Gaelan exchanged frightened glances.

"We have strong reason to believe that this young dinosaur is a seer, and has had visions of the future."

"I was right," whispered Azaria to Gaelan.

Polaris continued. "We must all keep watch for any of these signs, especially the Ishmael, and to report it to your leader immediately. But most importantly, stay close to one another, for if any of you is harmed, you will need someone close by to cure you."

"Cure you? What does he mean?" Azaria said to Gaelan.

"I don't know." Gaelan shook his head.

The herds listened and nodded, mumbling amongst themselves.

Mohala silenced them once again with her loud, raspy voice. "Unicorns, the great chief has spoken, and we must all vow to fulfill his wishes."

The unicorns chanted in unison, "We *will* fulfill his wishes. We *will* fulfill his wishes. We *will* fulfill his wishes."

Again Mohala spoke. "And now, many full moons have passed since our herds last came together. I suggest that we all take the time to enjoy one another's company." Her aged face nearly cracked when she smiled. "Let us begin the revelry!"

"Wahoo!" cried Azaria, galloping toward his friends. Springing into action, the four foals bolted to the river's edge. Gaelan pounced into the water, dousing his buddies with cold water.

"I'm going to get you for that," shouted Azaria.

He galloped quick as lightening toward Gaelan, only to be smacked in the face with icy water. Cassi and Jemmi laughed so hard tears streamed from their eyes. The fillies jumped in too, and soon they all ran and splattered each other along the river.

The sound of thudding hooves made them all turn.

"Hey, it's Zackary and Nathaniel," shouted Azaria at the arrival of his two cousins. "Hi you guys!"

The two newcomers didn't stop to greet them. They plowed right through the river, soaking the other foals.

"Why you..." shouted Gaelan, taking off after them, his long legs shortening the distance between them fast. Nathaniel and Zackary's loud whinnies pierced the air. Gaelan passed them, spraying them with his back hooves.

The young unicorns frolicked, pushing each other under the water, giggling, and stumbling. Soon their sides were heaving and they stopped, gasping and laughing at the same time.

"I have a good idea," said Nathaniel as he caught his breath.

"What?" the fillies both asked at once.

"Let's go spy on the grownups," he said, mischief glinting in his eyes.

"I don't know…" Azaria began.

"Yeah!" the others shouted.

They crept toward the adult unicorns, careful to make a long arc around Mohala. Hiding themselves behind some bushes close to the mares, they eavesdropped.

"Cassi and Jemmi are so fast. They're such tom colts," bragged their dam.

The two fillies turned and smiled at each other.

Dorianna, Nathanial's dam spoke up, "Well, you should see how quick Nathanial can gallop. He's definitely the fastest of the colts in *our* herd."

Nathaniel cleared his throat a little and wagged his head from side to side as though he might burst with pride.

"Well, my Zachary is a close second, though," claimed his dam.

Zachary turned and smirked at Nathaniel.

"Well, Gaelan can beat any other colt if he had the chance," bragged Elissa. "You've all seen his long legs. He's made for speed."

Azaria frowned. "Hey, no one is saying anything nice about me," he growled. "I'm outta here. I'm gonna go listen to the males."

The foals followed close on his heels, creeping only on the soft, silent grass to where the stallions were speaking.

"You know, I once ate some crabgrass and I was sick for days," said an elderly male.

"I tried an apple once," added a chubby fellow, "and it was mighty delicious, but the gas afterwards? Phew! What a smell!"

The foals stifled their laughter.

"I wonder what the new plants will do to us all, eh?" Someone guffawed.

"I don't know, but it can't be as bad as Clarence when he ate that apple!"

The males fell, rolling and hee-hawing with laughter.

After the laughter died, Orpheus, the ancient unicorn, renowned for his story-telling, spoke. "Well, I once journeyed to the dinosaurs' valley myself, and what I saw, was enough to make anyone's hair stand on end."

The young foals came out of hiding and gathered around Orpheus, knowing it would be an exquisite tale.

Orpheus began. "It was a night much like this one, when the full moon rides across the night sky. I knew it would be dangerous traveling on my own and was aware of the strange night beasts that attack tender unicorns when they're alone, but I was young and thought myself invincible. I made it to the valley with little effort other than my own strength and agility, and was met by the great chief. We spoke of many things, and I soon grew very comfortable as the grass there was mighty sweet, and I was enjoying a small feast. But the chief noted the shadows were growing long, and gave me fair warning. He said, 'Beware. There have been strange things carrying on at night, and eerie sounds heard. You should leave before nightfall.'

"I immediately rose, but the sun fell faster than I expected. I couldn't turn back because I knew the little mare wanted me home, so I kept going. As I walked, I was relieved the sounds were just the normal night noises one hears on a summer's eve, and I soon lost all worry. But when I came to an escarpment, I heard a voice. Soft at first, it grew louder and louder. It was like the moaning of a mare in great pain. I stopped dead, my heart pounding in my chest, and nearly turned to flee. But then I thought, 'It's probably just another unicorn. I'd better go save her!'"

Azaria sat up and moved his head forward to listen more intently.

"It was a terrible cry—the sound of gurgling and rasping as though someone was badly injured. I called out to see where she was. There was no answer, just the moaning, so I continued to search until suddenly, to my horror, I saw her. She was floating off the ground and, like a shadow, I could see right through her. She was..." and then his voice dropped to a whisper, "a unicorn ghost!"

His audience gasped.

"I wanted to gallop away as fast as my hooves could carry me, but instead, I stood my ground and faced her. After all, I was strong and could certainly handle a mere spirit."

Orpheus paused to catch his breath. "She wasn't the terrifying spectre I'd always imagined a ghost to be. Her eyes were sad, and she looked ill. I asked her what happened and she replied, 'I came to the dinosaurs' valley many years ago, but became lost searching for the right trail that would take me home. And then I slipped and tumbled down an embankment, breaking my back from the fall. There was no one close by to help me, and so I died, and now I am cursed to haunt this place until the end of time.' And then she faded from my sight. My fur standing on end, I galloped home as quickly as possible hoping to forget it ever happened, but sometimes, late at night, I think I can still hear her cries of pain and her anguished words."

The unicorns gasped and sighed at the close of his tale.

Jemmi and Cassi crept closer to Azaria. "Did *you* hear any strange sounds when you were in the dinosaurs' valley?" asked Cassi.

"No, of course not," Azaria said.

"Yes," interrupted Gaelan, his eyes bulging. "A sort of a whooshing sound."

Azaria looked at Gaelan, confused, and then turned to the fillies, popping out his eyes too. "Yes, and a creaking and groaning sound too."

"Come to think of it, didn't we see something sort of white?" asked Gaelan, his voice rising and falling.

"Yes, I think so. And it kind of waved in the wind," said Azaria in his scariest voice.

The fillies backed away slowly, their eyes wide as cabbages.

"And I think it was trying to speak." Gaelan said, the corners of his mouth twitching into a hint of smile.

The sound of voices in the distance broke the spell.

"Hey, they're singing," cried Jemmi. "Let's go join them."

"Yeah," said Cassi, turning to leave.

The foals mumbled with excitement as they quickly settled in for the singsong with the other unicorns.

Dorianna, Nathaniel's dam, neighed in her high-pitched voice. Other mares whinnying soon joined her. The males added sneezes and rumbles to the rhythm. Together, they sneezed, rumbled, whinnied, and neighed, their unicorn voices carrying into the night. Other animals joined in, the wolves and jackals howling along, while the birds squawked their part to the song.

Azaria thought it was the most beautiful sound he had ever heard. He couldn't remember having had such a wonderful time in his whole life. He wished it would never end…but it did, all in an instant, when a loud hissing sound filled the air. The singing ceased abruptly as the unicorns looked up, their eyes filled with horror.

Chapter Four

The Great Fireball

"A giant fireball!" cried Azaria.

The unicorns stared in silence, mouths gaping.

Azaria stood, his eyes fixed on the huge rock burning and hissing as it hurled through the air toward the earth. Sparks flew everywhere, threatening to ignite the grasslands of the valley. The giant rock whizzed through the heavens until it disappeared from sight. The herd waited, but nothing happened. Several seconds later, a loud crash thundered far in the distance and the ground shook. Azaria's body slammed into a boulder.

The unicorns broke into panicked neighs.

"It's what the dinosaur predicted!" shrieked a male.

"There'll be monsters on two legs!" cried a female, her thin voice piercing the air.

Azaria struggled to get up. He pushed with his two forelegs, but a sharp pain shot through his hip.

"Mother," he called, "I can't get up...Mother?" He listened for the reassuring sound of her voice over the cries of the others, but couldn't hear her.

"What if there's another one?" screamed a hysterical mare. "The valley will burn!"

"Quiet! All of you," Mohala's thunderous voice shouted over the frightened crowd. "We are unicorns, *not* hyenas. You will *all* stop the hysterics." The noise subsided except for a few sobs. Mohala continued. "Now stand at attention and listen to Polaris, the Great Stallion."

Polaris appeared before his herd looking shaken, but still standing tall and proud. "Unicorns, I believe what we've just witnessed could be the beginning of the change young Darius spoke of. I hoped it wouldn't happen so soon, but here we are. And now we must be strong and stand united. We must swallow our fear, for it's our fear, not the fireball that threatens to destroy us. We have three strong herds and I know we'll survive this. Now let's begin by helping those in need, and from there, we'll decide what to do."

Azaria felt soothed, yet confused by his father's words. He struggled to rise again, but rolled back to the ground in pain.

"Father!" he called, "I'm here. I can't get up."

Within seconds, Aurora and Polaris were by his side.

"What happened?" asked Aurora.

"The earth shook so hard I fell on that sharp rock." He tried hoisting himself up again. "If I can just get up a little further..." He groaned. "I could maybe stand."

"Azaria, stay still," ordered his mother.

The colt tried again.

"Just stay still," commanded Polaris.

"No...I think I can..."

Polaris lunged at Azaria with his horn. The colt fell back frightened, but the horn settled softly on the very spot that stung. He yelped in pain.

"Stay still," Aurora repeated.

It came slowly at first—a warmth that grew hotter and hotter until it nearly burned. Azaria squirmed and, just as he was ready to cry out again, the heat subsided and along with it, the pain. Looking up, he saw his father grinning, one eyebrow raised as though they had just shared a very good secret.

"Feeling better?" Polaris asked.

"How did you do that?"

"A new lesson for you, my son," he said, laughing. "Healing! Something you'll be able to do once you get your horn."

"Me? Really?" Azaria rose slowly, testing his hip, astounded by the small miracle. Then something caught his eye. "Mother, that mare has cut her head and...oh look...that one's bleeding really hard! She's going to die."

He tottered to the first mare, still cautious of his injury.

"Just watch, Azaria," Aurora said, coming up beside him.

Again, he was dumfounded when his mother touched her horn to the wound. The gash in the mare's head miraculously sealed itself.

Azaria looked around at the scene of destruction in awe as the unicorns tended to one another. Ever so gently, Dorianna, Nathaniel's dam, ambled to the bleeding mare, and laid her horn on the gash. The bleeding stopped within seconds, and the mare calmly rose and joined the group.

"Now you know why we have to stick together," said his mother, "in case something happens. It's how we survive."

A feeling of brotherhood filled Azaria. "I never knew, Mother. It's amazing. It's…because we're unicorns."

"That's right." She smiled.

The unicorns continued one by one to find the injured among them, and to heal them. A gash on a leg became new flesh, a broken rib became whole, and a torn ear reshaped itself. They worked hard until near dawn when they finally huddled close together in exhaustion, far from the comfort of the banyan tree, to sleep.

Azaria trembled as he imagined what the change would bring. Something very large and ominous had struck the earth. Darius' words echoed in his brain. What did they mean? What would happen now? His thoughts whirled in his head as he fell into an exhausted sleep. Then, daylight crept in again like a cruel, twisted beast. It was the dawn of a new era.

Chapter Five

The Change

Azaria awoke to stinging nostrils. He coughed several times and opened his eyes.

"Mother," he called, "what's that smell? I can't breathe. There are clouds everywhere and I can't see very well."

"It's the change, Azaria," she said, her voice quivering.

Memories of the events of the night before jolted him. He turned in circles and stared, bewildered, at snow drifting slowly like wispy feathers to the ground. He had heard about this stuff, so soft and cold, and how it would fall to the earth from a grayish-blue sky when the air was chilly. But when he opened his mouth to catch some flakes, neither was it cold, nor did it melt on his tongue.

"This isn't snow, is it, Mother?" he asked, spitting out the dry, bitter flakes.

"No," she said. "It's ash. I've seen this before after lightning strikes. It's what's left over after things burn."

He remembered the sparks that flew from the fireball, and then asked, hesitantly, "Mother, where's the sun?"

"Gone," she said in a tiny voice.

"What happened to it?" he asked, his eyes growing wide.

"I don't know."

Waiting for her to nuzzle him and tell him all would be alright, Aurora said instead, "Just stay close to me and the herd, okay?" And then she turned away.

Azaria didn't like this new side to his mother. She had always been so strong and reassuring, but now she seemed almost as scared as he was. He rubbed his face on her soft cheek, but she wouldn't look him in the eye.

Scared, he turned and searched for Gaelan, who stood shivering close to his dam. His friend jumped, startled, when Azaria approached him from behind.

"Gaelan, there's something really wrong. The sun's gone!"

"I know. I heard the mares talking," Gaelan whispered. "They say it was the sun that hit the earth last night." His face crumpled and he burst into tears. "I'm scared. What are we going to do?"

Azaria was taken aback at Gaelan's tears. "I don't know." He looked around at the herd again, and then made up his mind. "Father told us not to be afraid, so let's just act like there's nothing wrong. Then maybe we won't notice it so much."

"Okay." Gaelan sniffed. "I guess if you can do it, I can too."

"Good," Azaria said as though he were Polaris himself.

In the weeks that followed, the world was cast in semi-darkness. Each morning, Azaria saw the skies grow lighter, but no warm sun shone through the cloud. Each evening, he waited in hope as the skies grew dim, but no stars or moon lit up the night. The white ash floated to the ground covering the grasses the unicorns needed to survive. They huddled together, scraping through the soot to find any bits of green they could. Most of what they found was brittle and dry, and so the herd grew thinner by the day. The river banks too were piled high with sludge as the river struggled to clean itself of the soot that had fallen like filthy snow into its life-giving waters. And sadly, the banyan tree where the unicorns gathered, grew grey and collapsed one dreary day.

What were equally bad were the nightmares Azaria suffered each night. Spectres of two-legged monsters invaded his dreams, and he often awoke, breathing hard and bathed in sweat.

"Mother," he whimpered one day, "will the sun ever return? I'm cold. I'm *always* cold. I just can't seem to warm up. And I'm hungry. I want food."

Aurora turned to her foal, her eyes tired and head drooping. "I know. We're all hungry. I don't think anyone could have ever imagined the change would be this bad," she said. "But you know, all bad things have to end. And this will surely end too. Remember what Darius said, that the plants would change?"

"Yeah," Azaria said, his ears pricked forward at the hope in her voice.

"That means that *something* will grow again, and soon we'll have food. And maybe we'll find another banyan tree for our gathering place. He never said that we wouldn't survive now, did he?"

"No," Azaria said, uncertain, "he didn't. But what about the creatures-that-walk-on-two-legs? I'm really scared they'll find us. It's hard to sleep at night."

"Don't think of those things. It'll only frighten you more. Put it out of your mind. It's the way of the unicorns."

Azaria knew her words were true, and that he had no choice but to find the strength. If for nothing else, at least for Gaelan.

Yet despite the dismal landscape and the doubt, the foals grew braver and still played as all young do in times of distress. Soon they drifted further and further from their dams. Sometimes it was to run to the river. At other times, it was to race further and further away in the grassland.

One day, the four foals wandered away to play a game of Hoof the Soot, a contest Gaelan had invented where the foals pushed ashes with their hooves to make piles.

"Let's see who can make the biggest pile," said Cassi.

"Mine's going to be high as a mountain," bragged Jemmi, sweeping cinders on her mound.

Azaria pawed at the ground, determined to win. He checked Gaelan's pile out of the corner of his eye. Seeing Gaelan's mound growing faster than his, Azaria pushed the ashes with all his might, kicking the soot backward faster and faster. Turning, he saw Gaelan look back and paddle feverishly. Azaria dug harder than ever. Then small wisps of sand began whipping in patterns around the heap.

"Who did that?" he called in an angry voice. "Gaelan, you're blowing away my dust pile."

"It's not me!" growled Gaelan, his accusing eyes falling on the twins. "It's the fillies!"

Azaria glared at Cassi and Jemmi, only to be met by confused expressions. His eyes wandered back to his pile. Grains of sand danced through the air as they swirled and rippled away from his mound. He watched, spellbound by the pretty designs.

"It's the wind!" he cried.

The four foals watched the sandy arabesque, fascinated.

Then Gaelan made a discovery. "You know, this wind is getting so strong, I think I can fly."

"Me too," Jemmi said, springing forward.

29

The foals abandoned their game, leaping higher and higher. "Hey, look at me," cried Cassi. "I'm practically flying!"

"Me too," said Jemmi as the wind caught and lifted her..

But soon the delicate breezes took on an ominous new twist.

"Ow, that stings." Cassi pawed at her eyes with her foreleg.

"What's happening?" cried Gaelan, rubbing his smarting eyes against his chest.

"I don't know. We'd better get back to our dams," called Azaria. He peered in the direction of the mares, but saw only a blur. Terror seized him. "We shouldn't have gone so far!" he shouted. "It's all your fault, Gaelan. It was your idea to come out here."

"Not it wasn't. It was Jemmi who said we should do it," snarled Gaelan.

"Was not," Jemmi shot back.

"Was too."

"Never mind. Let's just go," Azaria shouted.

He led the way, calling for Aurora. The four friends pressed forward, their eyes tearing as the winds grew stronger. Nearing blindness, Azaria panicked. Soon, large drops of rain pelted down to add to their misery.

A loud crack filled the air.

"Watch out!" shrieked Gaelan as a large branch crashed down, nearly striking Jemmi. The filly's frightened screams pierced the air.

A strong gust of wind knocked down Cassi. Azaria and Gaelan stopped and pushed her back up to a standing position.

"I don't think we'll ever get there," cried Cassi, tears streaming from her eyes. "I'm just not strong enough."

"Yes, you are," yelled Azaria above the noise of the wind. "You're a unicorn."

"Yeah, but I'm just a filly," she wailed.

"Fillies are strong too," shouted Jemmi.

And that's when Azaria heard it—the call, weak at first, but very real.

"It's Mother!" he exclaimed.

His strength renewed by the sound of her voice, he plunged forward, the other foals close on his heels. They struggled toward the faint sound. Soot, sand, and rain whipped at their coats, burning their skin. Plowing ahead, they listened for Aurora's muted call until Azaria saw the dim forms of the mares huddled before him. They rushed forward to meet the foals.

"Quickly, we must find shelter. The cave is over there," ordered Aurora, her voice choked.

"Where? I can't see," shouted Azaria over the din.

Aurora pointed her horn in the opposite direction. Azaria couldn't make out the cavern, but put all his faith in his mother. They pressed through the hurling winds staggering as they went, their eyes closed in slits.

Then the screaming winds grew muffled. Opening his eyes a little wider, Azaria looked around. Smooth stone walls surrounded him. It was very dark, but he knew they had arrived safe inside the cave.

He listened to the savage howls of the winds that tossed the lands about. "It's so loud, Mother. When will it stop?" he asked.

"I don't know, Azaria," she said, her voice shaking.

Fear filled him again at his mother's uncertainty. After all, hadn't Mother always fixed everything before?

The foals huddled with the herd, listening to the storm. No one played and no one spoke. They fell into a fretful sleep until a loud neigh awakened them.

"The winds are dying down," shouted Mohala.

Azaria sprang from the floor of the cave and strained to see. It was true. The winds had abated. The storm was nearly over.

The unicorns shuffled about the cave, nickering until the skies grew calm again. Then, one by one, they left the cave.

Azaria stared in disbelief at the devastation. The storm had been so powerful it had uprooted trees and flattened them like twigs, leaving a desolate landscape.

"Look," cried Gaelan. "The winds blew away a lot of the soot. Now maybe we can find food." He leapt out, his long legs pounding the earth as he galloped.

"Gaelan, come back," shouted Elissa.

"Food! Food!" cried the unicorns. They darted out onto the plains, prancing and leaping, wandering further and further from the cave.

Azaria sprang forward too.

"No, Azaria. Let's wait," cried his mother. "I don't think it's safe yet. I've heard of storms that sleep and then reawaken."

She was right. Within minutes, the storm surrounded them once more in all its fury.

Azaria and his mother fled back into the cave, Elissa close behind. The frantic whinnies of their fellow unicorns fighting to return pierced the air.

Azaria noticed the worried expression on Elissa's face.

"Mother, what if Gaelan doesn't come back?" he whispered.

"That's what I'm worried about. We've got to help him," she said. "Try calling him. Your voice is higher than Elissa's and will carry further on the wind."

"Alright, Mother. I will." Standing as close to the mouth of the cave as he could, he called and called, but nothing happened. He looked back at Aurora.

"Try again," she said.

Azaria raised his voice as high as he could and called even louder.

Something big flew into the cave, a tangle of legs, rolled around a couple of times, and then clambered up on all fours.

"Gaelan!" Azaria exclaimed.

"Phew, that was close!" Gaelan gasped for breath.

"What happened?" asked Elissa, her eyes moist with tears.

"I ran out to get some grass. And then, when I saw the storm was starting again, I galloped as fast as I could. I wasn't sure if I was going the right way, but then I heard Azaria calling me, so I knew I was. And then, all of a sudden, I was here."

"It's those long legs that saved you," said Elissa, laughing and crying at the same time.

They waited and called a while longer, guiding the unicorns back. When all seemed to have arrived, the unicorns stayed put until they knew for certain the storm was really over. Remaining close for many days afterwards, no one ventured far from the shelter.

"Gaelan," Azaria whispered a few days later, "have you noticed there are some unicorns missing?"

"Yeah. I heard they were taken by the storm," said his friend in a hushed voice. "Some of the older ones weren't able to get back when the winds started again."

Azaria's heart fell. He remembered the group of older unicorns who hung together and reminisced about days gone by, particularly the males they had spied on the night of the revelry. Some of them were gone, and those who remained hung their heads in sadness.

He recalled his father's words that day on the mountain. The unicorns had no enemies save for the Rexus.

But what about the skies?

"Azaria, what if the unicorns don't survive the change?" Gaelan asked, his lips trembling.

"Polaris said we would and we will!" Azaria vowed, stamping his hoof.

This was not the last of the storms. They came and went, each time taking victims with them. Azaria was alarmed as the remaining herds grew gaunt, their ribs protruding from their sides from starvation.

Then one day, the skies grew brighter, the smoke thinned, and small seedlings rose from the ash. It was spring.

Chapter Six
Darius

Head held high, his eyes shining, Gaelan galloped toward Azaria, kicking his heels in the air. He gradually slowed and came to a stop right before him, his eyes lit up.

"You look pretty happy," Azaria said, amused. "What's up?"

"Ahhhhh, it's those delicious, tender shoots of grass coming up. They're so good. I just can't get enough of them." He pranced. "And did you notice? It's warmer and the sky is so much lighter."

"I know. And look how much we've grown. We're done with starving." Azaria wagged his tail. "And we're yearlings now! See? I'm getting my horn!" He bent his head down to show off the stub of his sprouting bud.

"Me too!" said Gaelan, bowing his head to reveal the small growth. "Did you know the other day I actually healed my mother when she scratched herself on a dead branch? It was a little difficult because my horn isn't very long yet, but I did it."

"I did too," Azaria exclaimed. "I healed Jemmi when she fell and twisted her ankle. I had to practically stand on my head to do it, but it worked."

The colts threw their heads back, shaking their manes as they laughed. Then Gaelan grew serious.

"Azaria? Have you noticed there are no new foals?" he asked.

"Yeah, I did. Mother says when there's no food, there are no foals. It's the way of nature."

"Really? But what if they never have any again?"

"I don't know. Father says we need foals to survive. Otherwise everyone will just grow old and die," said Azaria.

Gaelan thought for a moment. "Too bad we can't talk to Darius. He would know what's going to happen."

"Yeah. But he's pretty far away, and it's not really safe yet. And there's still the Rexus." Azaria cocked his head. "I know! I could ask my father. After all, he *is* the leader of the herd."

"Good idea! And see if I can come too," said Gaelan.

"Alright." Azaria nodded.

That evening, he approached his sire, walking tall and straight, and holding his head high.

"You look so grown up," said his father. "I almost didn't know it was you.

The colt's mouth curled up in a proud smile.

"Father, I think we should go the other valley and see if Darius has been having any of his spells," he blurted out. "I want to know what's going to happen next."

Polaris sighed. "I've been thinking that too."

"Seriously? So we can go?" Azaria tried his hardest to contain his excitement.

"Well…I'm just afraid of what I might find. The dinosaurs are huge animals, and I'm not so sure they fared well."

"But can we at least go see?" Azaria pleaded.

"I don't know." Polaris looked away.

"After all, it's for the good of the unicorns." Azaria put on his speaking-to-Saul voice. He waited. When he thought Polaris might not answer, he turned to leave. Walking no more than a few paces, he heard his father call.

"We'll see."

"Yes!" Azaria exclaimed, leaping into a gallop. He ran to tell Gaelan the news, cantering in circles around him.

"Did he say *I* could come?" asked Gaelan, joining his friend's frolicking.

"I don't know. I forgot to ask, but if he says we can go, I'll ask him for you too."

The next day, Azaria's chance came when Polaris stood before the herd. "I've decided I'm going to find Darius," he announced.

Sighs of relief resounded throughout the mares.

"May fair weather go with you," an older mare called out.

"And may you find Darius in good health," cried a male.

"I'll do the best I can," said Polaris, nodding.

Azaria leapt forward. "Father, I want to come too."

"I don't think so, Azaria. It's too dangerous."

"But Father, it'll be dangerous if *you* go alone. You were the one who said we should all stay together in case something happens. And we could bring Gaelan too. After all, you did teach us both how to speak to the dinosaurs."

"It's true, Polaris." Aurora said. "You shouldn't go alone. Azaria and Gaelan have shown a lot of courage during these hard times. I think you should let them go. And besides, what good will they do around here?"

Polaris eyed the two eager young yearlings. "All right," he said. "Let's go."

The trip was vastly different from the first time they made the trek. Vicious storms had uprooted the once-majestic trees, and windfall littered the ground. The stench of mold and rot invaded their nostrils while they trudged through the mire. Large puddles stretched their long arms around the terrain like claws, making the journey all the longer as they navigated around the deep waters. The worst part was the mosquitoes that tormented the unicorns. They shook their coats repeatedly to rid themselves of the annoying insects that feasted on their blood.

Hearing the pitiful sound of a mournful bird crying for its mate, Azaria recalled the fright they encountered on their first trip. "Better watch out for the flying dinosaur," he joked. But none came. He glanced around. "Gosh, they're no birds around for real this time."

"No trees to build their nests in," Polaris said, looking back.

Azaria frowned.

They trudged through the mud until at last they arrived at the opening of the valley. Though he was tired, Azaria's pace quickened. But when they rounded the corner, his heart fell. It was far worse than he had imagined. Hundreds of skeletons and bones lay on the ground where dinosaurs had breathed their last breath.

"They're all gone!" cried Gaelan, his eyes wide with disbelief at what had become a massive graveyard.

"You were right, Father."Azaria's voice trembled. "They just didn't have enough food."

He fought to keep the tears back. He wouldn't cry—he just wouldn't. Looking about, he wished that somehow Saul would make an appearance, that somehow there had been a mistake, and that just around the bend he might come upon the long-necked dinosaurs. Scanning the skies again for flying dinosaurs, he found nothing.

"Let's keep looking. You never know. There may be survivors," said Polaris, squinting as he searched.

"Maybe we'll find some further in the valley," said Azaria, his voice choked.

"There aren't even any Rexus," said Gaelan.

Azaria couldn't imagine that a beast as powerful as the Rexus could be beat.

They explored the valley for what seemed hours. It was the same everywhere—bones, dead trees, watery fields infested with mosquitoes, and stench. No animal life, save for a few birds chirping forlornly, and the odd field mouse.

"We may as well go home, Father." Azaria's voice quivered. "There's nothing here."

"I think you're right," said his father.

They turned to leave when a movement caught Azaria's eye. Fearing the Rexus, he raced to catch up to his sire, his coat breaking into beads of sweat. Then his heart leapt, for there cautiously moving toward them from behind a large boulder was Darius.

"You're still alive!" shouted Azaria, dashing to his friend.

"You finally came," cried the half-grown dinosaur, his voice cracking. "I've been waiting so long. Quick! Come and help!" His eyes threatened to spill over with tears. "There's something wrong with my mother."

The unicorns followed the distraught dinosaur to a secluded spot in the damaged terrain. There lay Maresa, emaciated and gaunt, her skin rough and scaly, and her eyes glassy. With great difficulty, she raised her head, and sighed with relief.

"Polaris! Oh, how I hoped that someone would come to help us. It's been terrible. There wasn't enough food. We're the only ones left, and I'm afraid I'm too weak to move on," she said, her voice feeble.

"You must try. Come with us to the unicorns' valley. Already the sky is lightening and the sun will return, and then there'll be new trees for you to feed on," Polaris promised, a false note in his voice.

"No, it's no use. There won't be enough trees or ferns anywhere for a long time," she said. "It's just too far and I'm near the end, but please...please take Darius. He's much smaller, and I know he can survive."

Darius's face was streaked with tears. "No Mother! NO! I won't leave without you!" He placed his mouth gently over her neck and tried to pull her up, but Maresa's head was too heavy. He lost his grip, and her head settled on the dirty ground again.

"I can't. I'm too weak. Only one of us can survive, and it won't be me. Please go on, Darius, and save yourself. You were given the gift of sight for a reason. You must carry on." She broke into a fitful cough.

Sobbing, Darius struggled to pull her up again and again. Each time she fell backward. She tried to cough once more, but her lungs only rattled. Then she settled down and drifted into a deep sleep. Darius, tired too, lay down beside her and was soon asleep.

Several hours passed. The dinosaurs dozed on. Maresa's breathing grew labored, and she mumbled from time to time.

"I'm afraid it won't be long now," whispered Polaris. "We'd better stay with her through the night."

"But Father, why don't you just heal her?" Azaria fought back the tears.

"I can't. It would take a whole herd of unicorns to heal an animal this size," he said. "Our healing powers are only meant for each other. And besides, we can't cure starvation."

Azaria withdrew, sulking, and then moved close to Gaelan. "She doesn't deserve this," he whispered to his friend, trying to keep his voice steady. "She was so kind and gentle. Why doesn't this sort of thing happen to bad creatures like the lions?"

"A lot of lions didn't survive either," said Polaris. "We've all lost members to the change. All we can do is try to go on."

Azaria blinked several times. He remembered his mother's words and whispered them to himself over and over. "All bad things must come to an end. All bad things must come to an end," as though somehow his words would make it all go away.

The unicorns stayed by Maresa as the evening air grew colder. Where once the night had been rich with sounds, there only remained the ghostly sound of the wind whistling over Maresa's labored breathing. It reminded

Azaria of Orpheus' story the night of the great fireball, making him shudder. He looked down at Darius sleeping on the soil.

The small dinosaur awoke and wandered over to his mother as she took her last breath. He gazed down at her, his eyes filled with tenderness.

"Good-bye, Mother," he said. He looked up into the dark sky at the millions of twinkling stars and spoke, his voice mysterious and songlike. "Can you feel her?" he asked. "Can you feel her spirit leave?"

Azaria shivered, and then exchanged looks with Gaelan.

Darius stared at the sky for a long time, a slight smile on his lips. Then he turned to the unicorns as though the spell had been broken and said, "While I slept, I had a dream of what the future will bring. My mother was right – I must carry on. I'm ready to go with you now."

The unicorns rose without question and led the young dinosaur home.

Chapter Seven
Close Call

Azaria's wide eyes took in the sight before him. Grasses had reclaimed the land and large, leafy ferns magically transformed the drab browns to rich greens. Great ponds, that had tormented him with mosquitoes, had long dried up. He looked to where the grey trees had fallen. Now saplings shot up, and the forest promised to return. It was the sky, though, that captured his attention that morning, making him feel giddy.

"It's the sun. Can you see it through the haze?" he called, swaying back and forth, his neck stretching toward the heavens.

"Ohhhh!" cried Gaelan. "So it didn't hit the earth that day. It was something else."

"I guess not." Azaria paused, and then gave a mischievous smile. "But I knew all along that it would come back."

"You did not, you big phony!" Gaelan sideswiped Azaria.

"Yes I did." Azaria shoved him back.

"Did not," scoffed Gaelan.

"Okay, so I didn't." Azaria bowed his head, feeling sheepish. "But I'm glad it's back. We need lots of it to grow ferns for Darius."

"I know. Have you ever seen anyone eat so much in all your life?" Gaelan looked back at the dinosaur in the distance.

"No. He's grown to twice his size since he came to live with us."

"Yeah, I know. My mom says we didn't know what we were getting ourselves into."

"Nope, but he's a lot of fun, though. He's really changed the valley for the better," Azaria said.

He looked further to where Darius played with the unicorns. The giant beast picked up Cassi gently in his mouth and placed her on his back. Cassi teetered forward along his bony spine. She squealed with delight when Darius lowered his tail, and slid to the ground. In the same way, he lifted Jemmi. Other unicorns lined up for their turn, laughing and giggling as they scrambled.

Azaria remembered the day they returned with the much smaller Darius. How the unicorns gaped at the strange creature and darted out of the way when he trundled into the herd until Polaris, Azaria, and Gaelan appeared.

The stallion trotted up, and announced, "This is Darius. His dam passed away early this morning from starvation. He'll be part of our herd from now on."

His words had been met with incredulous stares, but within days, they all warmed up to the giant beast, and he became a popular playmate for young and old alike.

"Hey, Darius, let's play hide and seek," called Azaria one day.

"Yeah," shouted Cassi, "but you'll have to find us again since you're so big and can't hide."

"Dinosaurs can hide," replied Darius.

"No, they can't," said Gaelan, "unless there's a mountain nearby."

The young unicorns laughed together, enjoying the joke.

"Don't be too sure," Darius began in a low voice. "Sometimes they can sneak up on you…quite suddenly!" He leapt forward, scattering the foals, and landed with a loud, rumbling thud.

"Yeah, but you're the only dinosaur around, and you can't hide from us anyway," said Cassie, laughing. "You're too big."

"No…I'm not the only dinosaur," replied Darius, his eyes staring off into the distance.

Azaria's ears pricked up at his words. He felt his hair rise on end, but he quickly forgot it as he was caught up in the swiftness of the game.

"Okay, then. Let's play," said Cassi. "Azaria, you're it."

"Ah, not again." He turned his back, counted, and then turned around to search for them.

Where's Darius?

He wandered around to the usual hiding spots, finding Jemmi behind a dead log, and Cassi hidden behind a large stone. Joining forces, the three searched together for Gaelan, discovering him hidden in the crevasse of a stone escarpment.

"Where's Darius?" Azaria asked.

"I don't know," said Jemmi.

Cassi shook her head too.

"Gaelan?" He eyed his friend.

"He was here a minute ago."

They looked about.

"Darius," called Azaria. "Where are you?"

There was no answer.

"Darius?" they called.

"He's too big to hide anywhere," said Cassi, twitching her ears.

"What if something's happened to him?" asked Jemmi.

"What could possibly happen to a huge dinosaur?" Gaelan's asked.

A loud thud made them jump.

"Looking for me?" Darius looked pleased with himself.

"Where were you?" cried Cassi, her nostrils flared.

"Didn't I tell you dinosaurs could hide?" Darius chuckled.

"Yeah, but how?" asked Gaelan.

"I just can." Darius said, grinning.

* * * *

One day the yearlings wandered far away from Darius and the herd.

"Oh look," cried Gaelan. "A cave. Let's go explore it."

"Well, I don't know…" began Azaria, remembering Saul's warning.

"Oh yeah, let's!" squealed the fillies, breaking into a trot.

"But…what if…" Azaria broke off.

"What? Are you a mouse?" teased Gaelan. "Afraid of the dark?"

"Well no, but you remember what Saul said about the caves," Azaria said.

"But Saul's gone. Remember? The fireball? All that stuff?" scoffed Gaelan.

"Well, alright."Azaria surrendered.

He followed the girls and Gaelan into the cave, their hooves clattering as they tread on the hard rock. Azaria knew that this had probably once been a lair of the Rexus, but didn't want to be left behind.

"It's really dark in here," said Jemmi, her voice unsure.

"Yeah, it's like night," agreed Cassi, looking back to the mouth of the cave where daylight still shone.

"Hey, I hear an echo!" Gaelan cried.. "Echo…echo…echo…"

43

The fillies joined in too. "Hoo…hoo…hoo…" called Jemmi, throwing her head back like a wolf.

"Tweet…tweet…tweet," chirped Cassie, pursing her lips into a beak.

Then Azaria heard it—a long scraping sound almost as though a very large unicorn was dragging his hoof slowly across the floor of the cave.

"Listen, you guys!" he whispered, his hair standing on end. "Did you hear that noise?"

"What noise?" asked Cassi.

It came again, louder this time. Scrape, s-c-r-a-a-a-a-p-e.

"That one," said Azaria, breaking into a cold sweat.

"Stop doing that," ordered Jemmi. "You're scaring me."

"Doing what?" asked Gaelan.

"That," replied Jemmi.

"I didn't do anything," Gaelan's voice rose in pitch.

"Well someone did," Jemmi whimpered, looking back and forth in the dark.

"Quiet," Azaria said.

The yearlings froze. The ominous sound came again, only this time longer and slower…and much closer. Azaria jumped.

"Darius, is that you playing a trick on us again?"

The sound moved closer.

"Darius?"

Scrape.

There's something else inside this cave! Let's get out of here!" he cried, scrambling. The unicorns bolted from the cave. The scraping sound grew stronger and faster. Leaping into the light, they galloped for several lengths before Azaria dared to look back. There, to his horror, a monstrous grey Rexus stumbled toward them growling fiercely.

"We've got to get to the herd," he cried.

Azaria looked over his shoulder again, and then slowed to a canter. "Look," he said, "It's starving! It's really sick and weak."

Bones protruding through its skin like skeletal branches of a dying tree, the Rexus hobbled toward them. Through glassy eyes, it stared at the unicorns, drool slithering from its mouth. Singling out Jemmi, it staggered toward her, snagging its claw on a rock, and nearly fell. Jemmi screamed. The Rexus snapped its huge jaws, and the young filly ducked to the side. It tore at her with its razor-sharp claws, but she leapt away as it lurched forward.

The herd came thundering from afar, shouting threats at the Rexus, Darius close behind.

"They're too far. They'll never get here in time," shouted Gaelan.

Azaria stared at the scaly monster, unable to move. He opened his mouth to scream when a loud noise startled him. Turning, his eyes opened wide at the sight of Darius.

"Darius? How did you get here so quickly?" he asked.

Darius ignored him and faced the Rexus.

"Look! He's going for Darius!" shouted Cassi. She closed her eyes.

Darius remained perfectly still.

"Oh no you don't, you old bunch of bones," yelled Polaris, closing the distance between them. He lunged at the Rexus and tore through the great beast's heart with his horn, ripping the shriveled skin as though it were mere lichen. The Rexus stared down to see its scarlet blood oozing from the wound. It spun around, gazed up at the sky, and then toppled to the ground dead.

The unicorns trembled in the aftermath of the attack, breathing heavily, their faces etched in fear. Tears rolled down Jemmi's white cheeks.

"Haven't we suffered enough without this?" she sobbed. "So much has happened. And now this. What if there are more Rexus?"

Jemmi's dam moved closer to soothe her, but it was Darius' words that calmed her.

"There aren't. I'm the last of the dinosaurs," he said, his voice gentle.

Azaria was stunned to see how composed Darius was as though nothing had happened. He stepped forward. "You weren't the slightest bit afraid, were you?" he asked, his head cocked to one side.

"No," replied Darius, lowering his head to Azaria's level.

"But why not?" asked Gaelan. "You could have been killed."

"Because I knew it wasn't my time," Darius replied, looking back and forth at the members of the herd. "I haven't fulfilled my life's task yet. You see, I'm going to live to be very old."

Mumbling broke out as the unicorns digested his words.

"But you're the last of the dinosaurs. Doesn't that make you sad?" asked Jemmi, her tears drying.

"No, because I have all of you."

The herd was quiet for a moment. Then one of the mares spoke. "And we're glad we have you too."

Laughing and crying at the same time, the unicorns moved forward and laid their horns affectionately on Darius' sides. Darius returned the gesture by touching them with his nose.

Azaria stood back from the group, feeling glum as he watched them turn to leave.

He heard Cassie call out in the distance. "Hey, how come Polaris can kill with his horn? I thought horns healed?"

"Because he was angry," said a mare.

"So when you're angry your horn can kill?"

"Yes, it's very powerful." Azaria could scarcely make out the mare's voice because they were so far away now.

Azaria didn't follow. He had noticed the leaves on the trees growing thinner, and that there were fewer ferns.

Certainly not enough to feed a long-necked dinosaur.

Bowing his head in sadness, he decided to keep what he knew to himself—that Darius would soon have to move on to find food.

Chapter Eight

New Arrival

Azaria stood in the cool river, the chilly water tickling his lips. Gaelan, Nathaniel, and Zackary splashed about close by.

There had been talk of the other unicorns joining Polaris' herd. The leaders had said they'd be safer in greater numbers. Zackary and Nathaniel, his two cousins, had been with them for days, and Azaria hoped they would stay as each day had been packed with adventure.

Drinking deeply, he flinched when something sharp struck his nose. Jerking his head up, he watched as a strange object swept past him and floated into a small backwash.

"What was that?" he asked, turning to his friends.

"I don't know," said Gaelan, moving forward and cocking his head to one side. "It looks like it's made of trees."

"Yeah, but I've never seen anything so straight coming from a tree," said Azaria, wrinkling his brow.

"It's weird," Nathaniel said, following close behind Gaelan and eyeing the piece of wood. "Why don't we ask Darius? He'd probably know."

"Good idea," Azaria agreed. He stretched his neck and searched for the dinosaur. "Where is he?"

"Probably looking for food as usual," said Gaelan, craning to see as well.

Catching site of Polaris, Azaria called out, "Father, look. What *is* this?"

Polaris narrowed his eyes, and poked at it with his hoof. The thing dipped down in the water, and bounced back up. He pushed it with his nose only to have it drift away.

"I really don't know! Mohala, what do *you* make of this?"

The ancient mare waded into the water and touched the object with the same results, shaking her head in bewilderment. Soon all the unicorns were circling about, eyeing it, touching it, and talking about the strange thing found in the river.

Feeling a sudden rumbling of the ground, Azaria turned to find Darius.

"There you are. Darius, what do you think this is?" asked Azaria

Darius lowered his head to see, his expression changing to one of terror. He backed up two steps, breathing in large gasps. "A box!" he whispered. Twisting around his massive body, he broke into a run.

Azaria followed, calling, "Darius, what's wrong?"

"They're coming!" Darius said, rivers of sweat pouring off him.

"Who?"

"The creatures that walk on two legs!" the dinosaur called back, his voice trembling as he sped away, his powerful legs shaking the earth.

Azaria broke into a canter. "But you said all the dinosaurs were gone. The Rexus' are dead. They can't bother us anymore."

Darius looked back as he fled. "These creatures are far more dangerous than the Rexus, especially the Ishmael. You have no idea. You simply have no idea at all! I've got to hide."

Azaria watched his friend flee. He looked back at the herd for a moment. When he turned back, the dinosaur had vanished.

He stopped, mystified. "Darius, where did you go?" he called.

All he heard was the forlorn whistle of the wind.

A few days later, they came. Azaria and Gaelan's ears twitched nervously as they watched the large floating boxes they traveled on, land.

"The creatures-that-walk-on-two-legs are actually strange," said Gaelan. "Kind of small too."

"And they're hairy, but they don't have pelts like the other animals. And did you notice the males have manes like lions but not the women?" asked Azaria.

"Yeah, they look like monkeys!" Gaelan broke into a chuckle.

"Only bigger. And they're carrying something on their bodies that doesn't fall off," Azaria said, eyeing the false skins they wore.

One of the creatures, who always seemed as angry as a Rexus, made garbling noises while pointing to the giant floating boxes. The others listened, and then unloaded them.

"Hear the noise they make? It has patterns. Do you think they actually have a language?" asked Gaelan.

"I guess so."

They watched from afar while the beings unpacked their belongings, taking them out of yet other boxes. The angry creature who ordered the others seemed to be in charge. Within a few days, they were making long, hard box-like objects from the sand that they piled one on top of another. One full moon later, a small group of straight cave-like dwellings had sprung up on the banks of the river.

"I didn't know you could make things like that with trees and sand," said Azaria, his eyes large.

"But how do they do it?" Gaelan frowned.

"It seems they have hands that can hold things." Azaria stared down at his own hooves like he had never seen them before.

"Just like monkeys," Gaelan repeated his joke-grown-stale as though it was the funniest thing in the world. He laughed himself silly until Azaria gave him a stern look.

"Think maybe Darius is wrong?" asked Azaria.

"I don't know. They look pretty harmless. To tell you the truth, I don't think they're even interested in us."

"Probably because they have those other animals—those things that Mohala calls big-hooves," said Azaria.

The unicorn-like creatures that accompanied the humans fascinated Azaria. They were larger than the unicorns, but came in several different colors and had huge hooves! He wondered if that was what gave them their great strength when they pulled heavy loads. Stranger yet, was that they actually obeyed the creatures-that-walk-on-two-legs! When the creatures ordered them to move, they did. When they insisted the big-hooves stop, they did that too. Azaria simply couldn't understand why these beasts lived and worked when they could be free like the unicorns.

Then one day, the creature who seemed in charge sat down in the long grass and watched the unicorns, entranced. He stayed there for the entire day, only to return the next day, and the next day after that.

"He's too close." Azaria let out a nervous rumble.

"But he's not doing anything," said Gaelan, swatting flies with his tail. "A lion attacks quickly after seeing its prey."

"Yeah, but these aren't lions." Azaria scraped his front hoof nervously.

"But look at them. They don't move fast and they don't have sharp claws or teeth."

"If Darius said they were dangerous, I believe him," insisted Azaria, loyalty burning fierce in his heart.

"I guess time will tell."

Several weeks later, it almost seemed as though it *had* when Polaris addressed the herds.

"Some of you have been concerned about the creatures-that-walk-on-two-legs and wondering what we should do. I've been watching them now for quite some time. They haven't made any advances on us. So I think we can all relax and live in harmony with these creatures as we have for generations with other animals."

"But what about Darius' words?" called Azaria. "He told me they were worse than the Rexus."

"Yes," added Aurora. "And he's been right about everything else."

"But he fled before even seeing them," Polaris said. "It could be another creature, much larger that walks on two legs and hasn't arrived yet. But honestly, I don't think this is it." The other mares mumbled in protest. Polaris continued. "But just so you'll all feel comfortable, I've decided that our herds will stay close together in case Darius' words turn out to be true. Even though we'll be three herds, it'll be as though we are one. That way, we can protect one another."

Nathaniel, Zackary, and Gaelan exchanged excited glances.

Azaria felt uneasy as his father dismissed the group. He had always followed Polaris' words blindly, but this time he was sure his father was wrong.

Chapter Nine

Ishmael

"They're lovely." Ishmael raked his fingers through his dark beard as he sat, mesmerized by the beauty of the unicorns. "Just lovely. This could be just what I've been looking for all along."

The asteroid's terrifying arrival had deeply affected Ishmael. His town had lost many people to the devastation. Hundreds had died of starvation and others of the diseases that snuck in like a thief to rob the folk of their loved ones. Ishmael's home like many others' had been swept away like sticks by the great hurricanes, leaving his family destitute. What was far worse than the desolation was what it had done to change the townsfolk. Ishmael had seen honest people marauding, stealing, and beating others for food. Tempers flared and people attacked neighbours for a mere morsel. At first Ishmael had been horrified, but then decided that he, like the others, had to survive no matter what the cost, and so he had hardened his heart. After all, this was the way of the new world.

He had gathered up the survivors and argued with them that there was no other choice but to leave and start again elsewhere. At first the townsfolk resisted, but his silver tongue convinced them. They built rather modest boats, packed up their meager belongings, and grudgingly set forth to find the new site, one where they could again prosper.

It had been hard. The boats were not solid and the humans not sailors. Several of the vessels were lost including two of Ishmael's. The townsfolk had floated down the river for weeks. When they finally arrived in the unicorns' valley, that gloriously warm day, it seemed like a paradise. The sun shone brightly, the storms had abated, and all was lush and green.

"This is where we'll start over again," Ishmael declared to the survivors, acting as their leader. He stole a glance at his wife, Adiva. She looked away, her lips pressed together in a tight line.

Ishmael gazed greedily at the unicorns. Wanting wealth and respect, he had never been content to simply grow his crops and survive off the land. He was no farmer. Having been a merchant before the asteroid, he sold goods until there were none to be had. Before leaving, he had gathered up several horses left to fend for themselves, the owners being too unwell to take notice of their livestock. Transporting these large beasts on the small barges to the new valley proved to be no small feat, but he managed to carry about a dozen of them safely.

Glancing at his small herd, he shook his head with impatience. "It'll take years to breed these horses," he said aloud to himself. "I want riches now. I want everyone in the streets to turn their heads when I walk by."

Ishmael turned his attention back to the graceful unicorns that grazed before him. At first their beauty had mystified him. He had sat and watched them gallop through the valley, their shimmering manes and tails flowing in the wind; their spiral horns, like jewels, ornamenting their heads like crowns. How majestic they were! How extraordinary! What great beasts of battle they could be if trained to use their horns as swords against their enemies' horses. He could become a general, leading his unicorns in attack against some future foes all the way to victory. The town would hail him a great hero, and he would be the envy of all.

As the sun lowered in the sky, Ishmael rose to his feet. It was decided —he must have one.

"Utterly beautiful…and very valuable indeed!" he said, his crooked nose wrinkling up into a greedy sneer.

Chapter Ten

The Capture

The thundering sound of hooves and the strong smell of sweat woke Azaria.

"Polaris, wake up!" neighed Nathaniel, bathed in foam, his sides heaving as he galloped into the herd. Dawn was creeping in. Azaria shivered at the crispness of the air.

"What is it?" Polaris grumbled.

"He captured them!" Nathaniel brayed. "He captured all of them!"

"Who?" Azaria heard his father demand.

"It's the creature-that-walks-on-two-legs, the one who kept watching us. He surprised us before dawn! There were several of them…they came out of nowhere! I'm the only one who escaped." Nathanial wheezed between ragged breaths.

"What's happening?" the mares mumbled as they began to stir.

"What has he done with the unicorns?" Azaria asked, racing to his father's side.

"The creature chased everyone into some…thing. It's like trees tied together. Once you're in, you can't get out." Nathaniel gasped for more air.

"Show me where!" Polaris roared.

Nathaniel reared and turned to go, and then stopped. "But, Polaris," he said, his eyes crazed, "I haven't told you the rest."

"What?" Polaris halted in mid-stride.

"The other humans…they call him Ishmael."

The great stallion's eyes grew fearful.

"I knew Darius was right," whispered Azaria to Gaelan who had crept up beside him. "I knew we couldn't trust the creature-that-walks-on-two-legs."

Polaris looked gravely at Nathaniel, and then glanced at the mares, calculating. "Then we'd better wait until we've studied the situation. Stay with us, Nathaniel, and be one of *our* herd. In the meantime, we'll have to come up with a plan to help Solomon. Azaria and Gaelan, you'll be our messengers and will communicate back and forth between our herds. As for the rest of you, stay far away from the creatures-that-walk-on-two-legs. Do *not* let them come anywhere near you. Understood?"

The unicorns whinnied in agreement. Their voices rumbled about what happened until the sun rose, softening the nightmarish feelings of the capture. Then they began planning.

That night, Polaris, Azaria, and Gaelan snuck on quiet hooves to the tied trees that Ishmael had built.

"How strange," said Azaria, eyeing the structure. "It really is all made out of trees."

"Stay back," ordered Polaris. "It's still daylight inside the creature's false cave. We'll wait until he's asleep."

Azaria was very curious about the strange light that the creatures-that-walk-on-two-legs created inside their dwellings. Stretching his neck out, he looked a little closer at the tiny fire burning on a twig.

Why doesn't it burn quickly like a stick does?

They waited until the moon traveled higher in the sky before Ishmael finally blew out the flame. Then they crept out of hiding.

They circled the tied trees, examining them from every side to see if there was some way out. The captured unicorns nickered their story in low voices as they rounded the structure.

"You must help us," cried Dorianna, Nathaniel's dam. "We can't get out."

"If there's no way out, then how did he get you in?" asked Azaria.

"There's a part of the tied trees that opens up," said Solomon pointing his horn to the end closest to Ishmael's dwelling. "They tied it shut after they herded us in."

Azaria eyed the mysterious spot, tilting his head to one side, then the other.

"It seems to me," said Polaris, "that we need to get Ishmael to open it for us. Does he ever open it?"

"Not so far," said Solomon.

"Then keep watching," Polaris instructed. "See what you can learn. We'll be back tomorrow to find out anything new."

Azaria, Polaris, and Gaelan bid the captured herd farewell and slipped into the dark of night.

The next day, they hid themselves in the forest close by. They waited some time and were soon rewarded when Ishmael strolled outdoors, whistling. He stood outside the tied trees, watching the unicorns with the same mesmerized look Azaria had seen before. After a time, he pulled out a long cord and climbed over the tied trees.

"A snake!" hissed Gaelan, shuffling his hooves and snorting.

"No wait. It's not. It doesn't have a head and it doesn't move," said Azaria.

"A dead snake?" Gaelan tried again.

"Gaelan!" Azaria gave his friend a friendly shove.

Azaria watched as Ishmael took the cord, tied the end and swung it around. The loop of the cord fell neatly over Zackary's neck and tightened. Zackary flinched, laying his ears back. He balked, shaking his head, and let out a shrill neigh. Ishmael held his ground, wrapping the end of the cord around a tied-tree. Then he ran to fetch another cord tied in different places that just fit the head of a unicorn. Moving forward, he tried to force it on Zackary's head. Zackary rumbled and sidestepped out of the way, shaking his head fiercely.

"You'll wear this halter if it kills me," Ishmael snarled.

The unicorn reared up and pulled back. Ishmael yanked the cord forward. They fought, unicorn against creature. Ishmael persisted and, after many tries, slipped the halter over the unicorn's head. Shaking his head with fury, Zackary lunged forward and dug his teeth into the flesh of the Ishmael's arm, drawing blood. Ishmael screamed, enraged.

Taking fast, hard steps, he retrieved a short stick with a cord attached to the end.

"You will do as I say or I'll whip you," Ishmael shouted, his voice hoarse with pain.

Zackary's hooves drummed the ground as he backed away again.

Raising the whip, Ishmael lashed out, cutting deep into Zackary's flank. His nostrils flared, Zackary bolted, zigzagging while Ishmael tried to steer him into a circle. The whip fell again. Zackary reared in protest. His eyes crazed, he broke into a gallop, dragging Ishmael behind him, the cord sliding through his enemy's hands.

Letting go, Ishmael pulled himself up and cursed at the angry, red burn marks in his palms. But Zackary wasn't done yet. Circling back, he reared and pummeled Ishmael's chest, knocking him onto his backside before galloping to the far corner of the tied trees.

"You stupid animal!" shouted Ishmael. "You're so dumb, no one can train you!" He hurled the rope and whip to the ground and stomped away.

Azaria giggled, his eyes watering. Gaelan joined him, and soon all three unicorns guffawed noisily.

"Did you see that?" asked Azaria.

"Zackary just wouldn't do what he wanted." Gaelan chuckled.

"I know!" Polaris roared.

They laughed heartily until Azaria suddenly stopped. "But that's it," he said. "That's the answer!"

"What?" asked Polaris.

That night, Azaria, Polaris, and Gaelan crept back to the captured herd.

"Friends," Polaris whispered.

Solomon trotted forward, followed by the mares. "You missed what happened to Zackary!" He shook his mane in disgust.

"We saw it all," said Azaria, breaking into fresh chuckles.

"Boy, was Ishmael mad when Zackary wouldn't obey." Gaelan chortled.

"Yes, well Zachary wasn't always the sharpest horn in the herd. I think he just didn't get it," said Solomon.

"Hey!" protested Zackary, scowling.

"But don't you see?" said Azaria. "That's the solution. If everyone were to behave in the same way, Ishmael would soon give up and set you free again. He would have no use for you."

Solomon thought a moment, his eyes shining with hope. "I think you may be right," he said.

The unicorns whispered among themselves, their voices rising and falling.

"But the whippings, Polaris, we're afraid of them. They hurt," whimpered Dorianna.

"Yes, but it only hurts for a moment," said Zackary. "It's not so bad when you know that it'll be healed instantly once Ishmael's back is turned."

"That's true," she said.

"I admire your valour, Zackary," said Polaris. "We should all be like you." He turned to the herd. "What Ishmael is really trying to do is make a bunch of big-hooves out of you! He wants you to obey just like them and carry creatures-that-walk-on-two-legs on your backs. And we're not big-hooves, are we?"

The unicorns broke into a fit of giggling. It spread like wildfire through the herd.

"Big-hooves are such dumb animals," one of the mares said, tee-heeing.

"They're total morons," said another, wiping her eyes against her side.

The laughter grew louder and louder until the door of the dwelling flew open, silencing them. Ishmael scowled as he looked around and saw the unicorns all huddled together in a corner of the pen. As the three free unicorns turned and fled, Azaria caught sight of an open-mouthed, wide-eyed Ishmael.

Chapter Eleven
The Boat

Ishmael fumed, slammed the door, and stomped into the brick house.

"They're brainless! I've tried nearly all of them and not a one is trainable. They're like zebras. Stupid, stupid, stupid!"

"You still have the horses," his wife Adiva spoke, her voice cold as ice as she chopped roots for their supper.

"Bah, horses. They have no horn. And they're not half as beautiful as the unicorns. They're as common as rodents. Now on the other hand, if I could train the unicorns," he said as though speaking to himself, "I would be the richest merchant in town."

Adiva hammered the knife onto the wooden cutting board, keeping her back to her husband, her long, dark hair trailing down her back.

"And what's with their hide? It heals the minute I'm not looking." He threw up his arms. "If I could find some way to make them feel more pain, then maybe I could control them."

Laying the roots aside, Adiva grabbed some cumin, threw it into a bowl, and ground it hard with her mortar. The scraping sound grated on Ishmael's nerves.

She cleared her throat. "Maybe you should try being a little more gentle. They're peaceful animals," she said, her icy voice digging in like a knife. She ground the cumin even harder, the abrasive noise growing louder.

Ishmael turned and glared. "What do you know about training animals? You've never even been on a horse. If I can't train them, no one can. I should just turn the lot of them out. They cost too much to feed anyway!"

Ishmael threw down his coat and stormed out of the room. His small daughter, Ali, cowered behind a chair, her brown eyes peering out as he moved past her. He had seen how the people snickered when he strolled past in town. In just a short while, he had become the laughing stock all because of those blasted unicorns. What could he do to regain the admiration of the people? Muddling it over in his brain for a while, he swung open the door and returned to his wife.

"You know, more people are settling in the town. If I could find someone dumb enough, maybe I could pawn the unicorns off on them. Then everyone would admire me for making such a smart sale." He laughed with scorn, wrinkling his nose.

"Or you could just be decent and let the unicorns go," Adiva said, lifting Ali to wash the child's face.

Ishmael's chance arrived one day when a boatload of people arrived in their small town. He waited as the vessel coasted slowly toward the quay, moving rhythmically with the waves that sloshed against the banks. It thudded against the dock with a dull sound. An odd, unpleasant smell he couldn't quite place drifted from the vessel. Craning his neck to see, he waited for the seaman to jump out and tie the boat to the deck, but the man never came.

"What the…" he said, climbing onto the craft, grabbing the rope, and forming the knot himself.

He hoisted himself up again on the wooden vessel, wearing his most polished smile, and peered in. It was dark inside and it took a minute for his eyes to adjust. Piles of what looked like clothes lay disheveled on the floor of the boat.

Something's wrong.

Moving closer, he jumped when one of the piles moved.

"Please help me," whispered a man, his voice little more than a rasp.

Ishmael's eyes fell on the black blotches of the man's arms. Jolting backward, he stumbled back onto the deck, his eyes wide with horror.

"It's the plague!" he shrieked. "It's the plague! They're all sick!"

Within minutes, many of the townsfolk surrounded Ishmael on the dock, all speaking at once.

"Get rid of them now before it spreads," screamed a woman.

"Quick before we all catch it," shouted a shopkeeper.

The mob crowded the boat. A young farmer with bulging muscles began shoving the boat out away from the dock while Ishmael struggled to untie it. Soon, several people were pushing too. The boat gave no resistance. It merely drifted away on the river, the waves lapping away in rhythm on its hull. The townspeople grew calmer as it moved from their sight. Turning to leave, Ishmael stumbled when two large, wet rats crossed his path, scurrying away.

Ishmael returned home, shaken by the ordeal. He scrubbed his hands and arms thoroughly with the soap Adiva made from fat and lye. His head ached from all the excitement.

"What happened?" asked Adiva, her brows furrowed.

"A boat came in full of dying people," he said, spitting with disgust. "They smelled awful and had black blotches all over their skin. I just can't get the smell out of my nose."

"The plague?" Adiva reeled, her eyes huge. "Did you touch them?"

"No, of course not. We just pushed them back into the river," he replied, the hairs on his arm standing up.

"You mean you didn't help them?" cried Adiva, her face a mask of shock.

"No. There was nothing I could do. We'd all catch it anyway." He shivered at the idea.

Ishmael had enough for one day and went to his room to rest for a while. His thoughts turned back to his herd of unicorns. He wondered if he could sell them as pets, but doubted it. Perhaps as meat? Shaking his head, he remembered the stomach sickness that struck after the fireball hit. The survivors had turned to other animals for food with undesirable results. He doubted anyone would sink their teeth into a new meat for a long time.

Two weeks later, Ali's whimpering woke Ishmael and Adiva in the night. Adiva felt the heat of her tiny forehead, gasped, and raced out the door to fetch reeds to cool the high fever.

"Can't anyone get some sleep around here?" grumbled Ishmael at the child's wails.

A few hours later, he awoke to find a distraught Adiva, her eyes dark from lack of sleep.

"She's throwing up now," she cried. "Go get the healer!"

Ishmael stared in horror at his tiny three-year-old daughter. He remembered the diseases that had gripped the entire town. Fear seized his soul. "Just keep cooling her down," he ordered, backing out the door.

Keeping away from the house until late that night, Ishmael finally crept in and shut the door with a soft thud. He slept near the hearth, away from Ali.

The next morning, he was awoken again when Adiva burst into the room, her eyes stained with tears.

"Look at her arm and legs!" She sobbed.

He looked at the child's limbs, his eyes round with horror. Bruises covered the little girl's body. Backing away, he nearly knocked over an urn over, and then sidled to the door.

"I have to tend to the unicorns," he cried, beads of sweat forming on his face. Throwing the door open, he ran to the corral, his wife in pursuit.

"It's the same thing those people had on the boat–the plague! You have to do something, Ishmael. Please help her!" she pleaded. "Go for the healer."

"No," he shouted, his voice shaking as he climbed over the fence. "He can't do anything for her."

"Ishmael" cried Adiva, still pursuing him, the girl in her arms. "She's our child. She needs help."

Ishmael hurried away, escaping the unpleasant sound of his wife's wailings. He stopped and stared, helpless from a distance, not knowing what else to do.

I can't get too close. I might die.

Hearing the dull thud of hooves, he turned to see a unicorn mare walk to Ali and touch the child's face with her lips.

"The mare…" he began.

Adiva looked up at the female whose warm head brushed against hers. The unicorn lowered her ivory horn and touched the dying child. Adiva gasped and tried to pull away, but stopped when Ali let out a giggle and reached her hand to the mare's face.

"It's so soft, Mama," she said smiling. She sat up in her mother's arms.

"Ishmael," Adiva squealed. "Her bruises and welts are disappearing. Oh, my gosh." She placed her fingers on Ali's forehead. "And she's cooling down too. I think the fever's breaking." She peeled off the child's clothes and examined the fading splotches. Then she looked at Dorianna as though a great revelation had come to her. "It was the mare!" she exclaimed.

Ishmael stood, his mouth wide open and the whites of his eyes showing. Then his expression slowly changed to a sly smirk.

"So, the unicorns have healing powers," he said, grinning from ear to ear. "And that's why when I whip them they get better so fast. They've been outsmarting me all along. I haven't been wasting my time with these creatures after all. I'm going to be rich!"

He leapt up, flailing his arms about, his eyes mad with glee, but stopped, noting the shock in his wife's eyes. Reaching over, he patted Ali briefly on the head and turned, his fast steps taking him toward the town.

Chapter Twelve
The Plague

The crying began in the settlement, first in one dwelling, then spreading to the next, each day growing worse. Azaria had once heard an old female sitting alone under a tree making this sad noise, but hadn't understood what it meant. Now he knew. He watched a male carry out a wrapped bundle, and lay it before the entrance. His mate joined him, and they both cried bitterly, their tears raining on the covering. Soon, more were left in the streets.

"The creatures are dying!" said Azaria, his voice low.

"I know," Gaelan said, his hide twitching.

"It's worse than the storms that took away so many of our herds," Azaria said. "I feel sorry for them despite what Ishmael did."

Gaelan shook his head. "But like Polaris says, it's part of nature, like when rabbits die out every seven years."

Gaelan pondered the drama before him for a while when his face lit up. "You know, maybe that's how we'll free the herd," he said as though he had just had the best idea ever.

"How?" asked Azaria.

"Well, Ishmael won't let them go now that he's figured out that unicorns can heal each other. But if enough creatures-that-walk-on-two-legs die, then he won't need as many unicorns anymore." Gaelan let out a stale laugh.

"It's not the other humans who did this, Gaelan. It's Ishmael. And besides, we'd still have to figure out how to open the tied trees." Azaria's smile was sad.

"True," said Gaelan, letting out a long sigh. He frowned, and then added, "But I won't forgive him for what he did to Dorianna!"

For days, they had watched Ishmael work with Zackary's dam. He had separated her completely from the herd, and then whipped her into submission until she allowed him to lead her around by a halter. He never let her return to the herd. Her back had remained streaked with blood, and her eyes were crazed with pain.

The next day, Azaria and Gaelan watched Ishmael lead Dorianna to the settlement. He took the mare inside one of the false caves and, a brief while later, guided her back out again. Cries of joy echoed from within the walls of the dwelling as Ishmael arose from the dark abode smiling gleefully, his hand clutching a small but dirty bag of gold.

Azaria's heart pounded. "He's using Dorianna to heal the sick, he exclaimed. "She won't survive!"

"She's only healed one of the creatures, Azaria," said Gaelan, his voice calm.

"Yeah, but remember Maresa, Darius' dam? Father couldn't heal her because she was too large. The same thing will happen here. She'll heal so many creatures that she won't make it. We've got to do something! We've got to find Father."

Azaria whipped around and broke into a gallop. They searched, but never found him. When they returned, all they could do was watch, their hearts sick while Ishmael led Dorianna from dwelling to dwelling, each time with the same results, the cries of joy and the filthy sack growing fuller and fuller.

"Look, Gaelan, her horn has changed colour. It's grayish," cried Azaria when the sun approached the horizon.

The two unicorns exchanged powerless looks.

Dorianna had slowed her pace. She staggered and then stumbled. Catching herself, she pushed forward, her eyes dull and listless. Taking a few more steps, she shuddered, and then fell. Ishmael grabbed her cord and pulled with all his might to force her up. The mare trembled, but couldn't rise. He shouted, and then pulled out the dreaded whip. She let out a hoarse neigh, her eyes wild with fear, struggled to her feet and traveled a few more steps, only to collapse again. Ishmael raised the whip, striking his mark, but this time she didn't move. He kicked her, but it was too late.

"She's dead," cried Gaelan.

"Oh my gosh!" shouted Azaria. "We've got to warn the others!"

The young unicorns galloped, their hooves thundering, to where they finally found Polaris and the herd. Azaria recounted the story, his voice quivering. The herd listened, stunned, and then broke into loud neighs and whinnies of grief.

"We must do something," cried a mare. "Otherwise, all the unicorns will die, and we'll cease to exist."

Azaria watched Polaris, his tail and ears twitching. The noble stallion had never looked so unsure or frightened in all of the yearling's life. The great leader looked helplessly toward the settlement, and pondered for a few minutes. Azaria thought he saw the glint of tears in his eyes as he turned away. Polaris faced the mares.

"Darius was right," he said. "Ishmael is far worse than the Rexus. I was so wrong. We're all in grave danger."

Chapter Thirteen
The Powder

Ishmael basked in the glory of a hero. He had single-handedly been responsible for the destruction of the plague. The frail townspeople held a ceremony for him and built a monument in his name. Women threw flowers at his feet, and the men honoured him with flasks of their finest wines. Ishmael strutted around for weeks until the townsfolk grew weary of his gloating, and he became just another man.

I don't get it. I saved the whole town from the plague and everyone's already forgotten about it.

He paced back and forth, fuming, before turning his attention to the sacks of gold sitting on his table.

"Hmmm! Nine bags for nine unicorns," he said aloud, counting his gold. "Let's see. It'll cost five bags of gold to pay for the new house. That leaves four." He dreamed of the envious looks the townsfolk would give when they saw his new home, but he was restless. Ishmael wanted more, and so approached Adiva.

"The men will begin the work on the house tomorrow," he said, breaking the icy silence of the room.

"So be it," she said, her voice void of emotion as she uncovered the rising bread dough.

Ishmael's muscles tensed at the coldness of his wife. "So what's wrong now? I thought you'd be happy being so rich."

"I would think a daughter and a wife and food on the table would be enough riches for anyone." She turned and pointed an accusing finger at him. "And you killed the mare that saved Ali. That was unforgivable." She thrust her fist hard into the dough, turned it over and punched it several more times.

Ishmael's face reddened at the memory of how he treated his daughter when she was sick, but it wasn't his fault. There was a plague going on. Anyone would have done the same.

"It's just an animal," he growled, his voice filled with sarcasm.

"No she wasn't. She saved your little girl's life. And for that, you should be eternally grateful."

Ishmael's cheeks burned with shame. He bowed his head for a moment, and then shook it hard. "Well, I think I know of a way to make more gold," he said.

Adiva didn't answer and kept pounding, but he persisted anyway. "There are nine horns. I could grind them up into a healing powder. Then I could go upriver and sell it for a fortune."

His eyes glinted at the thought of his fame in another town. His chest puffed out as he imagined the scene; more monuments, more flowers and wine, and best of all, more gold.

"And how do you know the powder would even work?" she asked, the tension in her voice as sharp as a knife. "Those nine unicorns died because they couldn't handle that much disease. I doubt there's any magic left in their horns."

"But there're always the others," he said, raising his eyebrows. "I could take *them* upriver."

"But you can't transport them. Remember how hard it was to get the horses here? These animals are far more intelligent. They'd escape."

"All the more reason to try the powder." He grinned wickedly, and then left the house.

He set out first to where Dorianna's skeleton lay along the path, but when he got there, he found two small bouquets of laurel laid by her bones. Puzzled, he picked up the bundles, stared at them, and then threw them aside. He sawed off the mare's horn from her skull and wrapped it in a dirty cloth. Returning home, he ground it to a fine powder. The horn smelled, so he threw in lavender for good measure. Next, he added some sweet clover to lessen the bitter taste. After several hours, he thought he had a finished product.

The next day, he marched into town, with purpose, his head held high. He walked past the monument where the flowers had shriveled and dried, where the streets now lay quiet. A few men raised their hands in acknowledgement, their faces void of any camaraderie as he passed them. Ishmael burned inside. No respect—he'd show them.

Walking as though he didn't care he, he made his way to the home of his old neighbour, Zeb. He knocked, but there was no answer. Pushing his ear to the door, he heard a weak call from within.

"Can't an old man get any rest around here?"

"Zeb, it's me, Ishmael," he said, his voice as sweet as strawberries.

"Away with you! I'm in rough shape today. My joints are just killing me. It hurts so bad that I can't even cover myself with a blanket. Not only am I in pain but I'm freezing too. I should have let the plague get me," Zeb shouted, breaking into the rattling cough of an old man.

Ishmael ignored Zeb's rudeness and shoved the door open. "Well, I have just the thing for you then."

"What? You got a unicorn hidden in that bag somewhere? I thought you killed them all off."

"No, my man," said Ishmael hiding his annoyance at the accusation.

"Well, that's what I heard," said Zeb, coughing again, this time much deeper.

"I have a few left. But I've got something better." He pasted on a phony smile.

"What?" Zeb croaked.

"Unicorn powder, made from the horn of a real, genuine unicorn. Guaranteed to cure you of all your ills," Ishmael said, enjoying his well-practiced sales pitch.

"Unicorn powder, you say?" The old man looked a little interested. "Yeah, but will it work?"

"Try it and see," said Ishmael, hiding his excitement. He removed one of the sacks, took a pinch of the powder and dropped it onto the old man's shriveled tongue.

"Aaaaaccccckkk! That's the worse stuff I ever tasted. What'd you put in there—horse dung?"

Zeb gagged and retched several times, but managed to swallow the foul mixture. When the gagging had passed, he lay back. A few moments later, his sour old face cracked like dried earth into a smile, and he sat up.

"You know, I think it actually worked. The pain's gone." He rose to his feet. "I feel new. This is amazing!" Walking about like a spry young man, his eyes glowing, he asked, "How much do you want?"

"Two pieces of gold for this sack full." Ishmael lured his prey in.

Zeb's eyes widened. His eyebrows slowly locked together. "That's a lot!"

"Well, that's my fee. Take it or leave it," said Ishmael, the corners of his mouth turned up in a grin.

"Ishmael, you know what I've always thought of you and your business dealings." reproached the old man.

"Take it or leave it." Ishmael's voice was firm.

"All right then!" Zeb roared, dropping his fist hard on the table.

Ishmael left the house, a broad, triumphant smile on his lips. He spent the rest of that afternoon harvesting the remaining horns. Again, he was puzzled when he noticed each skeleton had two small bouquets laid carefully beside them.

"Who's doing this?" he muttered to himself. "They're just beasts." He kicked the bouquets aside, scattering leaves everywhere. "The fools."

Chapter Fourteen

The Commemoration

"Let us commemorate those who died," said Mohala, her voice solemn and heavy with emotion.

Azaria listened as Polaris spoke first the names of those deceased, telling stories of each one, praising them, and shedding tears. Other unicorns spoke too, sharing funny anecdotes of their fallen friends. But after the laughter died, the humour merely made them lament all the more.

His head held low, Azaria remembered the last great meeting when they had all played and enjoyed each other's company. How things had changed. Gone was the freedom and simplicity of the life they once reveled in. Sure, things had improved since the fireball, but the one thing they couldn't fix was the presence of the creatures-that-walk-on-two-legs. They'd never leave., and they'd keep depleting the herds. Azaria sighed. How much more could they take?

Orpheus, the storyteller rose and asked to speak. Everyone grew silent as they did whenever he spun one of his yarns.

"My friends," he said, taking a deep breath, "I have a message for all of you—from the dead."

Azaria's mouth dropped.

"It's from the ghost of Dorianna," Orpheus barely whispered.

A mare gasped, while the others mumbled all at once.

"Oh stop your nonsense, you old big-hoof," cried one of the males. "Your stories are nothing but a lot of hot air."

"Yeah," cried one of the older unicorns, "This isn't a party. It's a commemoration."

"Leave him be!" shouted Azaria. "He may just be the storyteller, but he deserves respect too."

"Yeah, but it's not time for such shenanigans," cried one of the mares. "Ishmael desecrated Dorianna. He sawed off her horn."

"And all the others who gave up their lives for the creatures too," added a male, his voice rasping with hatred. "Who does Orpheus think he is anyway? Darius?"

Azaria raised his brows at the mention of the dinosaur's name. He cocked his head in thought, and then spoke. "Come on, let's hear him out," he insisted. "He's always good for a story or two. Besides, you haven't heard what he has to say yet."

"Oh, all right," grumbled the angry male.

The crowd quieted down. Orpheus cleared his throat and began his story.

"I was wandering down the trail where Dorianna died, when I saw a shimmering near her skeleton. I stared for a few moments thinking my eyes had a film over them. After all, I'm not young anymore, and eyes grow dim with age. But what I saw was real. My heart leapt and I turned to run, when I heard someone call my name. I stopped dead in my tracks and faced whoever or *whatever* it was. The voice spoke, saying that it was she, Dorianna, come back from the dead."

Their eyes wide, the unicorns moved in closer to listen.

"I couldn't really see her the way I see all of you now. It was more like looking through steam rising over a fire, only there was no flame. But I answered all the same and asked her what she wanted from me since I'm just the storyteller. She burst into tears and sobbed bitterly. I didn't know what to do. Should I console her? After all, she was a ghost. So I waited. When her tears dried, she said to tell her family that she loved them all and missed them, and that someday she hoped to see them again. She said it had really hurt to die when she knew she could have been saved, and how angry she was at Ishmael for killing her before her time. And then she told me something that sent shivers down my spine." He paused.

"What? What?" demanded the unicorns.

"She said…" he dropped his voice low, "'…beware of Ishmael. He is a ruthless creature with no conscience, and he has far more terrible things in store for all of you. Don't wait to see what he'll do next. You must *flee* him!'" His voice rose on the word flee.

Startled, many unicorns jumped back.

Nathaniel moved forward to speak. "If what you're saying is true, then we should destroy Ishmael before he destroys the rest of us."

The young males brayed and thumped their hooves in support of his words.

"Silence," cried Mohala.

The grumbling died down, but the faces remained sour.

"Violence is not the answer!" Polaris shouted.

"And why not? We can't do anything else. We're all just sitting here waiting for Ishmael to capture or kill us. And pretty soon, there won't be any unicorns left!" Nathaniel neighed fiercely.

Polaris' eyes lit up dangerously. "It doesn't matter what we do or how many humans we kill," he said in a venomous voice, "because not a single one of us can open the tied trees! And until one of you figures out how, stop complaining!"

No one answered. The tension cut like thistles.

"I think I may have a solution," Azaria offered, his voice calm.

The unicorns rumbled again for a moment, and then quieted down.

"Speak then and share your idea," said Mohala.

"Someone mentioned Darius earlier." He paused, and looked around. "And I think I know where he is."

The mares broke out into high-pitched murmurs.

"But surely he's dead." cried one of them. "There wasn't enough food."

"No, he ran away from Ishmael because he knew he was in danger. He told me he had a purpose in life, and I think that it has something to do with us. I'll swear by the magic in my horn that he's still alive and hiding out in the other valley. I can leave immediately and find him. I'm sure he'll know what to do."

The herd nickered with hope, and soon their voices rose in an excited chorus of unicorn chant.

"Let him go," they called out. "Let him go."

Mohala quieted them again.

"All right then, my son. You may go," he said. As Azaria turned to leave, Polaris whispered in his ear, "And fast before the herd turns violent."

Chapter Fifteen

Darius

Azaria had been walking for hours in the cold night air when the sun finally rose in all its promising glory. His shivering ceased when its rays warmed his body, and his pace quickened at the thought of seeing his old friend again. He imagined the look on Darius' face. Maybe the dinosaur already knew he was coming. Breaking into a canter, Azaria hurried until he spied the entrance to the valley. Then he stopped.

Suppose he hasn't survived. What if I find him dead like the other dinosaurs?

Scenes of the destruction of the fireball haunted him. He trembled with fear, and then, gathering up his courage, he rounded the corner, his heart thudding hard in his chest. He took a few more steps and… leapt with joy!

"It's beautiful. Oh my gosh! It's like it was before the fireball. The waterfalls—everything! And so green…except…the plants *have* changed."

A ray of hope filled him. Could all this lush vegetation mean that Darius was alive and well? He didn't have long to find out, for there a ways before him, stood the tall dinosaur, full-grown now, waiting for him.

"Darius!" Azaria sprang forward and danced around the huge beast, holding back tears of happiness. "I've missed you so much."

The lofty dinosaur lowered his head to Azaria's level. "And I've missed all of you," he said, his eyes watering. "But you have to understand that I had to leave. It was the only way. I have a purpose to fulfill, and Ishmael would have taken that away from me if he found me." He shifted uncomfortably. "It's been difficult being alone." Large teardrops plopped on the ground below, soaking it. The dinosaur let out a sob and gulped. "Why did you come here?"

Azaria took a deep breath and looked into Darius' eyes. "We need your help. "Ishmael captured Solomon's herd and killed several of our kin by using them to heal the creatures-that-walk-on-two-legs."

Darius thumped his tail hard, shaking the ground. "Did I not tell all of you he was dangerous?" his voice thundered.

"Yes, but I was the only one who believed you. Polaris and the others thought he was harmless, and that's why Ishmael was able to capture them. No one had their guard up—except me."

Azaria recounted all that happened. He told of the nine unicorn deaths and the desecration of the skeletons. He described the dilemma of the tied trees and the threats made by the younger unicorns.

Darius listened intently, frowning and pacing. "Fools," he complained, shaking his head.

"And now Orpheus claims to have seen Dorianna's ghost. She says that Ishmael has far worse in mind. And I don't know if Orpheus is just spinning one of his tales or if it's for real." He caught his breath and looked up pleading. "What can we do?"

Darius shook his head harder this time. "Ishmael is ruthless. He's driven by his own greed and his desire for power. The man won't stop until the very clothes he wears are woven of gold, and every one of the unicorns has been destroyed."

The truth of Darius' words struck Azaria with the force of one of Ishmael's whips. He broke into a sweat. "But there must be something we can do," he cried.

"There is," said Darius, his frown turning into a mischievous grin.

"What?" asked Azaria. "Tell me. I'll do anything."

Darius reached up to pull at some leaves high in a tree. He chewed on them before speaking. "You say Dorianna's ghost has been seen?"

"Well, so Orpheus says."

Darius finished chewing the leaves and swallowed. "Then, you must become a ghost like her."

Azaria jerked his head back. "Ghost? Me? But I don't want to die."

Darius chuckled. "You don't need to."

"How then?" Azaria frowned.

"Simple. You see my shadow?" the dinosaur said, amusement dancing in his eyes.

"Yes."

"Try and catch it!"

Azaria snorted. "I can't, Darius. Everyone knows you can't catch a shadow because it isn't real. It's just a play of light," he said, remembering his early colthood when he chased his shadow but never caught it.

"Exactly, and that's how you'll gain power over Ishmael," replied Darius matter-of-factly, "A ghost is like a shadow. And once you become a shadow, no one, not even Ishmael can capture you. Not to mention you'll scare the bejeebers out of him."

"Okay…" said Azaria, not convinced but still willing to listen.

"And if you can teach this to the others, the unicorns will have a far greater chance of survival."

"Alright…so how do I do this?"

"Easy. You must think like a shadow, move like the wind, and become a part of nature in a breath."

Azaria let out an exasperated sigh. "Well I don't know how to do that."

"Ah, but you can if you are willing. Are you ready to begin learning?" Darius asked, his eyes filled with mischief.

The unicorn paused a moment, and then replied with enthusiasm, "Yes!"

"Good. Now start galloping," Darius commanded.

Azaria smiled at Darius as though the dinosaur had just asked him to do something easy like chew on grass or breathe, and then broke into a gallop. He ran several circles around the dinosaur, and then came back, his eyebrows raised.

"Azaria, you're a fast runner, but not fast enough," he said.

"Well, I know I'm not the quickest in my herd, but I'm still *fairly* quick," said Azaria, his pride hurt.

"But you're still not as fast as the wind." He pointed his long neck toward one of the old Rexus caverns. "Gallop to the cave over there, but this time *become* the wind."

The unicorn flew. He kicked up his heels as high as ever, taking great leaps, and lunging forward. His muscles burned, and his lungs felt as though they would burst. He reached the cave, puffing and sweating.

"Well, how was that?" he asked, breathing heavily, his mouth drawn up in a proud grin.

"I don't think I've ever seen you run that fast," said Darius.

Azaria held his head high.

"But you were merely a unicorn galloping."

"What?" Azaria stamped his right hoof. "But that's what I am! I can't go any faster than that!"

"Ah, but you can. How do you think *I* got there so quickly when the Rexus was after Jemmi?"

Azaria shook his head. "I don't know."

"I *became* the wind. That's how. That means you have to be a part of it. You must feel its breath blow strong—and feel its power," Darius explained, his voice rising and falling.

Azaria heaved a sigh, and then pulled himself up to his full height. He waited, his senses piqued. A small breeze tugged at his mane and tickled his skin. It was cool and light, yet strong. Then he felt a gust, leapt, and…caught it! It carried him as he galloped. He was doing it—Azaria was riding the wind! He felt powerful. Excitement coursed through his body, and he nearly called out. But just as suddenly as he had captured the gust, he lost it and was galloping again. Slowing to a stop, he turned to Darius, his eyebrows raised almost to his ears.

"That was it, wasn't it?" he asked.

"It *was*," Darius' voice burst with joy. "And now you must continue to practice this daily until you're able to do it without thinking."

"You bet I will!" Azaria turned and galloped away to try again.

He spent the rest of the day practicing until he was exhausted, thrilled with his new power. He imagined the surprise of the other yearlings when they saw him race at this new speed. But remembering them also filled him with loneliness. And when night arrived, he collapsed into a deep sleep, dreaming of his family and the days before the fireball.

Two weeks passed—two splendid weeks in the valley with Darius. Azaria was certain he was the fastest unicorn that ever lived. He fantasized racing with the swiftest stallions, and of course, always winning. But something troubled him.

One night, he wandered to the clear pool of water where the bright moon's reflection glowed. He dipped his head into the cool water to drink when he heard a snap. A shrill whinny escaped him, and he hurdled backward, landing on his rump in the water.

Darius, close by, lowered his long neck. "Why so jumpy?" he asked, hiding a smile.

"I heard a snap. I thought it was a…" He paused.

"A what?" asked Darius.

"Well, a...a…a…"

"Azaria, you're a unicorn. You have no enemies other than the humans, and I'm here beside you. What could possibly scare you?"

Raising himself up out of the water and shaking off the drops, Azaria ignored the question and dipped his lips in the water, drinking deeply.

"Azaria?" persisted Darius.

"All right!" Azaria scowled. "I thought you were Dorianna's ghost!"

"What?" The dinosaur's head jerked back. "Dorianna's ghost? Why on earth would that scare you?"

"I...I...I'm scared she'll haunt me," he said, avoiding Darius' gaze.

Darius threw his head back and let out a loud chuckle. "But Dorianna was your friend."

"Yeah, she was," said Azaria, glaring at Darius, "But.."

"Then why should you be afraid of her in death?"

"Well..." Azaria tilted his head.

"The one who should be afraid is Ishmael. He's the one who wronged her." Darius grabbed some more leaves with his teeth and chewed them.

Azaria turned away, pondering Darius' words. "I suppose you're right."

"She's on your side," Darius said.

He thought a moment, and then said, "You really think so?"

"Definitely. Do you see me jumping at every sound because it might be my mother?" Darius smiled.

"No. Of course not." Azaria stepped out of the water.

"Well then?" The dinosaur turned his attention back to the succulent leaves.

Azaria breathed a sigh of relief and relaxed. He chuckled a bit at the silliness of it all and decided at that moment, he would never fear a ghost again.

The next morning, Darius quizzed Azaria. "What do you do if you see Ishmael and one of his men?" he asked.

Confident, Azaria shot back, "You become one with the wind, and flee as fast as possible."

Darius raised his brows. "That's one way, but there's another."

"What?" asked Azaria.

"You must be able to transform yourself into a rock or a tree, or anything that is near you in but a moment."

"How? I'm made of flesh and bones."

"Let me show you," said the dinosaur.

Azaria stood watching him when a large bird squawked nearby. He turned to look for only a second, and when he turned back, Darius had disappeared. Azaria looked about, turning a complete circle.

"Darius? Where are you?" he called. "Darius?" The dinosaur didn't answer. "Darius! This isn't funny!"

The unicorn trotted toward the cave, thinking for sure Darius had hidden himself inside, but stopped abruptly when he saw a portion of the cave transform itself into the familiar form of the tall dinosaur. Azaria jumped backward.

"How did you do that?"

Darius grinned from ear to ear. "I became one with the land," he said as though it was the easiest thing in the world. "Just like I did when we used to play hide and seek."

"But how can you? You're like me. You're made of flesh and bones."

"I just did and you can do it too. Try."

"You mean like this?" Azaria asked. He twisted and turned his torso trying to mimic a rock with a tree sticking up.

Darius began chuckling. Soon, he was rolling around on the ground, his huge body shaking the earth with giant spasms of laughter.

Untwisting himself, Azaria glared at Darius.

"What's so funny?" he asked, burning with humiliation.

"You, Azaria. You look like a unicorn pretending to be a rock and tree." He rolled and howled again.

Azaria fumed. Hot air snorted from his nostrils and his eyes bulged. "It's not funny!" he shouted. "I'm not a dinosaur. I'm a unicorn. I'm meant to run and play." He turned to leave in a huff, stomping his hooves hard on the ground.

Darius' laughter subsided, and he looked at his young pupil with softer eyes as he rolled his great mass up to his feet. "Don't go, Azaria. Times have changed. The unicorns *used* to run and play. But now they have to run and survive."

Azaria stopped. "Okay," he said, turning back to face Darius, his face knotted into a scowl.

"Try again, only this time, think of the cave and how it was formed. You are very old and have been there for thousands of years. Many seasons have passed; many animals have used you for shelter..."

Azaria listened, his eyes glazed as the words washed over him. He began whispering, "I am the cave, I am the cave, I am the cave." Visions of seasons passing—no—many seasons, hundreds of season, and animals coming and going, slid through his mind like water through polished stones. Then it happened. He felt his body reshape.

Azaria saw Darius' gaze pass right through him. The dinosaur looked about, then back to the spot again.

I'm invisible. He can't see me.

A bird cawed, startling Azaria. His concentration gone, he transformed back to himself.

"Was that it?"he asked, prancing. "Was it? Was it?"

"Yes! You did it. Now practice this some more and when you have mastered it, you'll be ready for the last step."

"I will." Azaria promised as he bounded away.

Chapter Sixteen
Fight and Flight

Ishmael sat at the table counting his gold, his face lit up like a bandit's lantern. He weighed the heavy metal in the palm of his dirty hands and proceeded to make several piles of coins, laughing to himself.

"Do you realize how much more gold we can make with the horn dust?" he asked Adiva, his eyes gleaming.

"No," she said, running warm water over Ali in her bath.

The little girl squealed at the sensation of the liquid tickling her skin.

"Far more than we did during the plague." He chuckled again. "Do you realize that if we slaughtered the rest of the unicorns in the pen, we could be rich beyond our wildest dreams?" His eyes narrowed in delight and his lips curved up in a nasty grin as he envisioned himself parading into town wearing rich linens and shoes made of the finest leather.

"What are you talking about?" Adiva stopped washing the child and flung around to face her husband, her wet hands dripping on her hips. "You're not going to kill those animals."

"Why not? I can't wait around for another plague, and I don't want to be dragging those wild unicorns all over town so people can touch their horns. It's easier this way."

Adiva took two quick steps toward her husband, her shoes scuffling against the floor. "But you'll kill them all and there won't be any left afterward."

"There's always the spring," he said. "There'll be more foals."

"But you'll kill them just as fast as they're born. How can you? Those animals were born to run free. You have to leave them be," she argued, her face locked in a frown.

"They're just animals, Adiva." He rolled his eyes.

"Mama, I'm cold," whimpered Ali, shivering in the bath water.

They continued to argue, their voices rising.

"Mama! I'm cold!" Ali cried again.

"Can't you keep her quiet?" growled Ishmael, his temper mounting.

"But you can't kill the unicorns," Adiva shouted.

"I'll do as I please," he roared.

"Mama!"

Ishmael turned and left, slamming the door..

There's nothing I hate worse than the wailing of a child, except a nagging wife.

He walked into town, searching for men whose hungry eyes spoke of desperation, men who would do anything he asked for a few coins and a supper. Finding several drifters whose dirty clothes hung in rags, he gathered them up and brought them to his home.

"Here's what we'll do," he explained. "We'll tie all the unicorns separately so that they can't reach each other. Then when I give the signal, we'll all shoot our bows at the same time and kill them all off. You must be sure they don't touch each other with their horns or they'll survive. It's the only way."

The hungry, ill-clad men nodded, stealing eager glances at Adiva while she prepared food for them. Ishmael noted the hard jabs of her spoon as she cooked, and how she slammed the plates with a thud, but ignored her.

After the men filled their empty stomachs, he sent them with their bedrolls to a small shed a short walk from the house for the night.

"We'll get up just before sunrise," he said before turning down the path to the house.

The next morning, the sun had already risen when Ishmael awoke.

"What?" he mumbled. "Why did I wake up so late?" He rolled over and sat up. The house was cold and the morning fire hadn't been lit. All was quiet. Not even Ali's little voice could be heard.

"Where's the child?" he said aloud. "Adiva? Adiva, where are you?" He paced around the house searching each room, confused. "She must be outside."

Ishmael swung the door open. He squinted, his eyes adjusting to the daylight. Then he rubbed them and looked about. Something was wrong. The holding pen…it was...

"What?" he shouted. "Where did they go?" His feet pounding, he ran to the shed where the men were bedded down and threw the door open. "What did you do with them?" he hollered. "I give you food and you steal my unicorns?" He aimed a swift kick at one of the men. Missing, he grabbed the man by the shoulders.

The man looked helplessly around at the others. "We didn't steal your unicorns. Look, we're all here. No one's gone. We've been here all night."

"Yeah, where would we put them?" asked another, coming to the first man's side.

Ishmael did a quick count of the men. Reality struck him full force.

"Adiva!" he shouted, his voice hissing with anger. "Where are you? I give you all the riches you could ever want and this is how you repay me? Adiva?"

The sound of the wind mocked him.

He tore into the house and stopped, seeing what he had failed to notice before. All his wife's things were gone, and Ali's too. On the table, lay a laurel wreath like the ones he found beside the unicorn skeletons.

"It was her! She's the one who's been laying wreaths beside the unicorn skeletons! She's been against me all this time!"

Ishmael threw over the table and chairs and pounded his fists on the wall.

How could my wife deceive me like that? My wife!

He covered his eyes with his rough hands and backed into a corner, sliding to the ground. He sat there for a while, and then slowly stood up, his face transforming to a nasty scowl as his thoughts took shape.

"You want to make a fool of me in front of the whole town, woman? Well I still have my men, and I'll hunt every one of those scrawny unicorns down and kill them. And you can't stop me."

Chapter Seventeen
The Shadow-Walk

"And now, Azaria, you have one final skill to learn. It's the hardest one of all," said Darius.

"Oh, good! What is it?" he asked, feeling very confident after mastering the other two skills.

"You must walk from here to that rock through the mud without making a sound or leaving any traces," said Darius as he shifted around his weight, making himself comfortable.

"Not a problem." Azaria grinned. He walked as quietly as he could, concentrating on the task and sure of success. But after only one step, he heard the unmistakable splitch-splotch of his hooves sucking up the mud. Looking back from the other side, his ears flattened, and he cried, "They're all there!"

"Ah, but not all of them," Darius said, a hint of smile touching his lips.

Azaria looked up, hopeful.

"Where are the prints of your shadow?" the dinosaur asked.

Azaria's face returned to its former scowl. "Well, there aren't any because my shadow's not real."

"But I distinctly saw your shadow follow you as you went along."

Azaria stared at Darius, utterly confused.

Darius continued. "Try again, Azaria, and this time, think as a shadow. Move as one. Be one. Shadows make no sound and leave no traces."

The unicorn scrunched his brows in deep concentration. He imagined he *was* a shadow, grey and misty, that he was light and airy, and began the walk again, this time riding on the tips of his hooves. He took only a few steps when one of his hooves scraped on a stone and he slipped, landing headlong into the mud. Struggling to rise, he lost his balance again, but forced himself up, grimacing at his muddy coat.

"Shadow, my eye!" he growled. "No one can be a shadow. Not even you. I bet you can't do it either!"

Darius pursed his lips and lugged his gigantic body up to stand. "Watch and listen," he said. His large feet shaking the ground as he moved, Darius plodded to the edge of the mud, and then placed one foot forward. When the other three followed, he transformed, floating, yet at the same time walking as though a spirit.

Azaria stood, his mouth agape. "How did you do that?"

"Simple. I was one with my shadow," Darius said as though nothing unusual happened. "You were not. You were imitating what you perceive a shadow to be."

"But…I…"

"Try again," said Darius.

"But…"

"Just try again!" Darius ordered, his voice firm.

Azaria let go. He stared at his shadow, his eyes glazed, and stepped into the mud, this time with his spirit. His body felt hollow and his mind was as silent as the stars. Feeling breathless as though he had lost matter, he began to glide. He moved with ease, stepping forward several steps, no sound—just he and his shadow. Elation filled him.

I'm doing it! I'm really doing it!

Excited, he quickened his pace only to hear the dreaded sound again – splitch-splotch. He hurried to the other side, spun about, and looked. There *were* a few hoof prints there, but most of them were missing.

"Darius? Darius?" he cried, his voice booming with excitement. "I did it for a few steps, didn't I?"

"Yes, you did." The dinosaur smiled so wide all his large molars showed. "And now you must continue to practice this until you can do it instantly. And once you can, you will be ready to save your herd."

Azaria gladly obeyed Darius, practicing for days. At the end of the week, he had mastered the near impossible skill. "I'm pretty good now, aren't I?" he asked, puffing out his chest.

Darius lowered his head to Azaria's height. "Yes, you've done well, but now it's time for you to leave.

Startled, Azaria stepped back a step. "What?" he asked.

"You must leave now," Darius repeated.

"But, I don't feel like I'm ready," he said. "I know I haven't always been polite, and that you were just trying to help, but I've been scared. Really."

"Azaria, you must leave now," Darius repeated again, his voice growing urgent.

"But, what if Ishmael is too strong, and I go back to find them all dead?" Droplets of sweat beaded his forehead.

"Your enemy has already been defeated. Ishmael has human foes too. When you return, you'll find your friends have been freed and reunited," he said. "But you must leave now; otherwise you *may* be too late. The herds are very angry and there'll be violence against the humans if you don't stop them. And if the unicorns attack the humans, the humans will destroy your species. So go now. You're needed."

Azaria stood undecided for a moment, and then turned, fleeing at a gallop. He sped up a knoll, but paused momentarily to call to his friend. "Good-bye, Darius. I'll be back soon, I hope."

"Good-bye, my good friend," Darius called back.

Chapter Eighteen
The Return

The day had turned somber when Azaria arrived at dusk. A heavy black cloud hung over the valley as though the skies would burst. He stood camouflaged on a ridge, watching the unicorns hovering together. Something was terribly wrong.

"It's a done deal," growled Nathaniel, facing off Polaris. "We're attacking the creatures-that-walk-on-two-legs tonight."

"No, Nathaniel! Violence is not the way of the unicorns," said Polaris, his voice strained.

Zackary shoved his face into Polaris'. "This is a new era, old stallion. You're not the one who sat locked in by the tied trees day after day wondering if you'd live or not. Every time that sun rose, we wondered if that would be the day we'd die and every time it set, we thanked the heavens we were still alive." Zackary bared his teeth. "I don't ever want to live through that again. It's time we did something."

"B-but at least wait until Azaria comes back," Polaris stammered.

How shrunken Father looks. So old. I hope I'm not too late.

"Azaria is dead!" roared Nathaniel. "Can't you understand that?"

"You don't know that for sure," said Polaris, moving back a step.

"A full moon has since come and gone," brayed Nathaniel. "He's not coming back."

Azaria spied Aurora standing close by, her jaw clenched in fear.

"No, tonight's the night. It's us or them. We'll attack the creatures and kill them off," insisted Nathaniel.

"I agree," said Zackary, moving next to Nathaniel.

"But at least wait until the next full moon," pleaded Polaris.

Nathaniel snorted in disgust, turned his back on Polaris, and moved forward, the other young unicorns falling in behind him, their fierce neighs ringing in a battle cry. "Not this time, old one. It's time someone got something done." He threw his head back, and gave his mane a savage shake.

It's now or never!

Azaria galloped to the herd, planting his feet firmly in front of Nathaniel. The unicorns squealed in fright.

"It's Azaria's ghost!" whinnied Jemmi.

"Oh, no! That's all we need—to be haunted on top of everything else," neighed Cassie.

The unicorns stood frozen until Jemmi finally whimpered, "Maybe he has a message for us."

"Message, my hoof," cried Azaria, a broad smile spreading over his face. "It's me—Azaria!"

"Azaria?" Their eyes grew twice their size.

"But how can that be?" asked Aurora. "You just appeared before our very eyes. No one can do that. You *must* be a spirit."

"No, mother. I'm *like* a spirit. Darius taught me how. Remember how he could hide and sneak up on us anytime even though he was huge?"

"Yes," Jemmi said. "I do."

"Well, that's what he taught me."

"What do you mean?" asked Polaris, tilting his head.

"Like this." Azaria disappeared, blending into the landscape.

"Where did he go?" cried Nathaniel, wildly looking about.

"Right here." Azaria laughed as he reappeared.

"But you vanished," Nathaniel said, his mouth hanging open.

"No, I merely camouflaged myself." He turned to Zackary. "Care to race?"

"I don't have time for this nonsense," grumbled Zackary, pushing past him.

Azaria darted to a nearby tree, in two breaths.

Zackary jumped back when Azaria appeared before him. He looked back to where he had been. "But...no unicorn can run that fast," he exclaimed, his anger turning to awe.

"You can if you're the wind." Azaria grinned from ear to ear. "Now watch. This is the best part."

He glided through a muddy stretch of trail while the others watched and listened.

"But there wasn't a sound," exclaimed Gaelan. "And no prints... what?"

Azaria faced the herd. "It's called the shadow-walk. I can teach all of you how to do this if you follow me. Then we'll have a much better chance of survival."

"But we've made our plans," said Zackary. His voice was beginning to lose its edge.

"Zackary, we've known each other since we were colts. Have I ever led you astray?"

The angry unicorn's expression faded, and he shook his head.

"Anger and hate will only cause more anger and hate. Come with me and I'll show you another way. We'll become shadow unicorns and defeat Ishmael together."

The young unicorns exchanged glances, and the whinnying subsided, the tension melting away.

"Okay, I'm willing to try," said Zackary, seeming more like the old Zackary from days gone by.

"Okay, I will too." Nathaniel snorted. "But if it doesn't work, we attack the creatures."

"And, by the way, they're called humans," Azaria said. "Darius told me."

"When can we begin?" asked Polaris, looking relieved.

"Immediately," said Azaria. "Night is falling. We'll travel all night to Darius' valley. And there we'll start."

The journey in the dark was long and hard, but when they arrived in the bountiful valley, Darius was there to greet them. Joy and hope ran through the herd as they reunited with their friend and wept tears of happiness.

The training began that very day. Azaria was a good teacher and had learned his lessons from Darius well. He taught the old and the young while Darius himself taught the vigilantes. By the next full moon, they were ready.

Chapter Nineteen

The Deception

Frustration swept through Ishmael as he prepped his cronies to ambush the unicorns.

"I know what I saw," said one of his men, breathing hard. "It was the ghost of a unicorn, and she was standing right next to where her bones lay!"

"Ridiculous." Ishmael waved the idea away. "There are no such things as ghosts."

"But I swear I saw the mare in the fog. She was beckoning me. I yelled and ran as fast as I could to get away!" The man's voice trembled.

"Did she follow you?" asked one of the other men, twisting his rope nervously around his fingers.

"No, but I just know something's going to happen. I think she was trying to warn me," replied the first man, squeezing his hands together.

"I've heard of others who have seen her too," someone else cried.

"Maybe we shouldn't go," said another man, his voice pitched high.

Ishmael knew he had to do something soon, or he would lose his men to superstition. His fortune had dwindled, and he was desperate to harvest more unicorn horns. Without the help of his men, his plans to take the powder upriver to the next town would die.

"It's just a trick of the mist." Ishmael shook his head. "There's been so much talk, that you're imagining things."

"I know what I saw if the gods be my witnesses," the man insisted, his eyes wide with fright.

Desperate, Ishmael made a quick decision.

"Okay, okay. I know you're all scared, but if you all come with me, I'll give each of you a cut of the powder when the job is done."

His offer was met with quiet, and then one by one, the men broke into smiles.

"Let's go," Ishmael ordered, leading his men to the saddled horses.

The men rose, grabbed their steeds and mounted them, falling behind Ishmael in the fading light of dusk.

They rode in silence, hoping to surprise the unicorns. The setting sun painted the sky a golden orange while the birds returned squawking from their feeding grounds to roost in their nests for the night. They had been riding for about twenty minutes when Ishmael spied the unicorns grazing in the sunset from afar.

"There they are!" Ishmael said, keeping his voice low. He whipped his horse into action, his heart beating fast. The men followed close behind.

Ishmael could almost taste the victory, as they galloped along. But when they got closer, the creatures disappeared.

He pulled up his horse, his men nearly catapulting into him from behind.

"Did you see that?" cried one of the men. "They're gone. Just like that."

"A trick of the light," Ishmael muttered. "Those large stones just *looked* like unicorns grazing." He scrutinized the land, scanning from left to right. "Let's keep riding," he said at last. Spurring his horse forward, he searched in the fading light, and then froze. Five lengths ahead of him stood Azaria, snorting and puffing. Ishmael sprang into action, but the unicorn disappeared again.

"Where did he go?" cried one of the cronies, his voice shaking.

The men looked about, dazed, in the increasing shadow.

"Follow its tracks," ordered Ishmael, squeezing his horse's sides.

They searched the ground as closely as possible in the fading light, where they had seen the unicorns.

"There's no hoof prints," cried one of the men. "It's gotta be a ghost!"

Ishmael descended his mount to examine the earth, when he heard a terrified shout.

"Look," hollered another one of the cronies, pointing.

There, floating before them, beckoning and whinnying in mocking neighs, was Azaria.

"I was right. They're spirits!" someone yelled. "It's the ghosts of all those unicorns Ishmael slaughtered! I'm getting out of here!" The man spun his horse around, whipping it into a gallop, the others close behind.

"Wait, you fools. They're not ghosts, I tell you. They're just unicorns!" shouted Ishmael.

His horse reeled and tried to break into a gallop. Ishmael yanked the reins, thwarting his mount from stampeding with the others. The horse twisted and lost its balance, throwing Ishmael from the saddle. Ishmael landed in a heap, and lost consciousness. Several minutes later, he awoke to the furious hoof beats of his horse as it galloped away. He sat up slowly, catching his breath, and gazed to where the unicorns had disappeared. The colours of the sunset had faded and with it the light, but there in the growing shadow stood the herd of unicorns, whinnying with glee.

"Spirits, my eye," he said with a menacing tone.

Chapter Twenty
The Hoodlums

Two full moons had passed since their triumph against Ishmael and his cronies. Though Azaria and Gaelan remained wary, the young, renegade unicorns began to show signs of cockiness.

"That was so funny that night. You were right, Azaria. They'll never catch us again," Zackary brayed as half-chewed grass fell from his full mouth.

"Yeah, remember Ishmael's men?" Nathaniel guffawed. "They were so scared."

"I know. They ran so fast and never even looked back." Zackary hoo-hawed, more chewed food dropping onto his white coat.

"I'm glad you tried it Darius' way," said Azaria, swishing the flies away with his tail. "If you had attacked the humans, it would have never ended."

"Yeah well, whatever." Nathaniel rolled onto his back and kicked his hooves in the air, scratching his back against some stubbly grass.

"Hey, guess what, guys? I heard some of the mares are with foal," Gaelan announced, smiling. "Now our herds will grow again."

"Mmmm," mumbled Zackary between bites.

"Yeah, I heard Aurora is carrying a foal. You'll have a little brother or sister soon, Azaria." Gaelan tilted his head in merriment.

"Yup. And next thing you know, *we'll* be the ones choosing mates," Azaria replied, a little embarrassed.

Something in the woods cracked. Azaria swung his head around, but saw nothing.

"Yeah, I noticed Jemmi's gotten to be quite the mare, eh?" Gaelan winked.

"And did you get a look at the mane on Cassi? What a filly!" Zackary brayed.

"Not for me," said Nathaniel, rolling over onto his stomach. "I've got better things to do."

"Yeah, right. Like what?" asked Azaria, swatting Nathaniel with his tail.

"Ah, you know…stuff," he said off-handedly, rolling to his feet.

As if on cue, Zackary piped up, his eyes bright with mischief. "Hey, Gaelan, a bunch of the guys were thinking of going into town tonight to scare the humans. Wanna come?"

"I'm in for sure." Nathaniel nodded.

"Not a good idea guys," warned Azaria, giving Zackary a piercing look. "Ishmael's a lot smarter than you think. I say we stay far from the town, keep them believing we're spirits."

"Oh, they'll think we're spirits all right," said Zackary tearing off more grass to eat. "I have no intention of spending time inside the tied trees again."

"You mean the fence, Zackary. That's what Darius called it."

"Yeah, whatever."

"No, seriously, Zackary, these humans are a lot smarter than you think and dangerous too. I wouldn't go anywhere near…"

Again Azaria heard a snap. He scanned the woods. A moving figure caught his eye.

"Human! Camouflage!" he ordered.

The unicorns blended into the landscape. They stood still, barely breathing until they heard running steps retreat.

Azaria was the first to transform back. "I don't like the looks of that," he whispered to Gaelan. "We'd better warn the others."

The young unicorns cantered through a scarcely used path unknown to the humans until they found the herd. Nathanial and Zackary trailed behind, guffawing and belching as they went. When they found the other unicorns, Azaria flew to his father's side and recounted the story.

"Father, I keep getting the feeling we're being watched, and I don't like it," he finished.

"I don't like it either. Sounds like Ishmael's up to no good and he's getting too close. I'll gather up the herd tonight and hide them among the dead trees. The humans are frightened of the grey forest," said Polaris. "I think they think it's haunted."

Azaria thought of the skeleton of forest that still stood as a dismal reminder of the fireball. "Okay, Father."

That night, as the moon rose and the jackals' howls filled the air, the unicorns lay low in the shadows of the dark and foreboding trees, like phantoms drifting in and out of the underworld. All was quiet except for hushed whisperings and the odd soft steps on the soil.

After a time, Azaria grew restless and sought out Gaelan.

His friend stood alone, mesmerized by the moon. "Remember the night of the fireball," he said. "It was a night like this we all sang with the jackals. How young we were."

"Yes, I remember. And we played with other foals in the water? Remember when Nathaniel and Zackary…" Azaria stopped in mid-sentence. "Speaking of Nathaniel and Zackary, where are those two idiots?" He glanced around.

"I don't know," said Gaelan, scanning the surrounding white skeletons of trees. "And where are the other colts from the other herds?"

Azaria gasped, his eyes wide with fear. "Do you think they went into the town like they said they would?"

"Oh my gosh!" Gaelan exclaimed.

"Let's go!" they cried together.

Plunging forward, they galloped at full speed toward the town. Sweat poured off their sides as they ran, and they snorted and puffed as they flew. They arrived close to the town in time to hear a blood-curdling scream.

"Look!" Gaelan pointed with his horn. "It's Nathaniel."

Below, a woman, her face twisted in terror ran for her life. Nathaniel followed on her heels, disappearing and reappearing while his mates guffawed.

"They're fooling the humans into thinking they're ghosts by camouflaging!" exclaimed Azaria.

Azaria sprang forward to stop them from further harm, but not fast enough. The renegade unicorns shadow-walked to the town square where several humans were gathered for a wedding. Zackary leapt through the group, wailing like a ghost, and disappeared. The humans panicked. They fled through the rows of tables, overturning them and spilling the carefully prepared feast on the ground. Nathaniel made for the bride and grabbed the hem of her dress in his big, yellow teeth. The dress tore with a loud rip as the shrieking bride struggled to escape. He let go with a loud whinny and joined Zackary, appearing and disappearing before the fleeing crowd. The mob ploughed forward into the streets, pushing and shoving, hurrying to the safety of their homes. They knocked over an elderly man in their desperation. The man cowered and called for help, but no one heard him. The renegade unicorns laughed cruelly.

Azaria waited until the last of the humans fled, and then dove at the young unicorns. "You fools! You idiots! Do you want us to be killed?" he shouted.

"Hey man, we're just having a bit of fun." Zackary chortled.

"Well it's not fun! You're scaring them!" Azaria neighed. "And someone was injured!"

"I don't care. They kept me locked up in the tied trees and I could have died. They deserve it!" sneered Zackary in return, his laughter turned to rage.

"You mean the fence. It's not them, lame brain. Ishmael was the one who captured you. These people are completely innocent. And the rest of you, following along like little lemmings. Unicorns are supposed to be much smarter than that! What's wrong with the lot of you?" Azaria roared.

The other unicorns stood, their eyes cast down.

"Ah, you think you know everything don't you? You're just like your old father. Always gotta be the good little colt. Aw, how cute." Zackary's mocking face changed into a scowl. "You'll never fit in with us. We're the new unicorns. We do as we please..." He turned to face his friends, but his expression fell when his mates moved to Azaria's side.

From the corner of his eye, Azaria spied the elderly gentleman struggling to pull himself up. He turned to Gaelan.

"I'll take care of it," said Gaelan. He walked toward the old man, his hooves clip-clopping on the stones in earthly fashion, and gently touched the trembling man's leg with his horn. The human cringed at first, but then relaxed at the sight of Gaelan's gentle eyes.

"You're one of the real ones, aren't you?" the old man smiled. "And you're healing me." The old man sat still as the heat coursed through his body. Then he rubbed his newly-healed leg and got up.

"Now let's go," ordered Azaria looking each unicorn in the eye. "If you want to stay here, Zackary, go ahead, but I won't let you put the others in danger."

The young unicorns turned to leave. Zackary sulked at the desertion of his fellow hoodlums and followed a short distance behind. They hurried along the trail avoiding Ishmael's house. When they neared the forest, a zinging sound split the air, followed by an ominous thud.

"I've been hit!" screamed Zackary. "Stop!"

Azaria looked back to see Zackary's face twisted in pain, an arrow buried in his flank, and a half-hidden Ishmael grinning from ear to ear.

More arrows flung through the air. Azaria dodged them."We can't. We've got to keep moving!" he shouted. "Fly!"

"But it hurts!" Zackary cried. "Please, Azaria, stop!"

The unicorns galloped furiously. Azaria checked back several times to keep an eye on Zackary who lagged further and further behind. After what seemed like hours, they finally stopped, their sides heaving. Zackary limped toward them, dragging a leg, blood pouring from his flank.

Azaria grabbed the arrow with his teeth and pulled with all his might, dislodging it, before touching his horn to the wound. The gash melted from sight. Zackary blubbered, his sobs racking his body.

"Not so tough now, are you?" Azaria snarled.

"I'm sorry. All I wanted to do was have a bit of fun. They think we're spirits, right?"

"Not anymore they don't," Azaria growled, "thanks to you. And to the rest of you too."

The young unicorns moped, not meeting his gaze.

"Now we're really in danger. Ishmael knows our secret and to make matters worse, you've all made enemies of the humans too. The whole situation far worse than it ever was. Now let's go!"

The unicorns shadow-walked into the forest, tired but relieved when they joined the rest of the unicorns. The mares exclaimed at the sight of the dried blood on Zackary's side, but Azaria said nothing. As far as he was concerned, they had dealt with the incident. All they could do now was wait and see how the humans would react.

Chapter Twenty-One

The Scorning

Ishmael strode through the spoils the townsfolk worked hard to clean. He stepped over rotting food and shook his head at the tables and chairs scattered everywhere.

Fools. All this over a bit of superstition.

Stopping at the square, he stared, smirking at the disarray when someone shouted.

"It was him," wailed an old hag, her wrinkled mouth opening to reveal rotten teeth as she cursed.

"It's his fault." An old man pointed his long bony finger at Ishmael. "You killed the unicorns, and now they've come back to haunt us."

"You ruined my daughter's wedding," roared the cloth merchant, his arms crossed and legs planted like strong pillars in the ground. "You should be driven out!"

The townspeople shouted and cursed at Ishmael as he pushed his way down the street. Still sure of himself, he maintained his proud stride.

Ishmael was quite pleased with himself. For two months, he watched the unicorns, always staying hidden in the deep recesses and cool shadows of the woods. Seeing them disappear at the slightest hint of danger, he noted they reappeared after it passed. He also observed they could change from their normal clodhopping pace to a silent, graceful, almost floating gait when spooked. But most revealing of all, he noticed they ate and left droppings just the same as any other animal. These weren't spirits! His arrow had attested to that when it drew blood from that big, goofy one.

"You fools," he cried. "They're not spirits. They've just learned a few tricks, that's all. Just like horses can be taught to pull a wagon, unicorns can be taught to hide themselves. I've seen it. I even struck one last night with an arrow. It bled just as any other beast would have."

"Lies! Lies!" cried the cloth merchant. "You've brought bad luck on us all. The whole town is cursed now."

Ishmael stood before the people, ready to fight when he saw a boy, his hands and face smeared with dirt, searching among the spoils. Sneering, the boy grabbed a bruised apple and flung it at him. Ishmael ducked, but the boy wouldn't be deterred. He aimed another apple at Ishmael's stomach with all his might. It struck him square on.

"You!" shouted Ishmael, groaning with pain. "I'll get you for that." He seized the boy's arm and yanked it. The boy screamed. Ishmael raised his fist, but stopped when he spied a small girl cowering in a corner against the rough bricks of a building.

Ali! My daughter. You're still here. But where is...?

And then he saw her. His wife stood cloaked in the shadows, fear etched on her face, reluctantly meeting his gaze.

"Adiva," he pleaded. "Where did you..."

Before Ishmael could finish his sentence, she hurried away. Ali ran to catch her mother's hand. Anger surged through Ishmael.

How dare she turn away from me. Who does she think she is?

Determined as ever, he faced the people."No! I tell you, they are made of flesh and blood just as you and I, and I'll prove it to you."

He spied two of his cronies who had crept out from the hovels and shelters they had constructed, silently watching the commotion. Their faces were gaunt and their skin sallow from hunger. Ishmael regarded them with new hope.

"You two! Come ride with me again. Find the others and together we'll capture some unicorns and bring back their horns to prove it."

"No, not their horns. You'll have to kill them first," shouted the baker's wife.

The angry voices of the crowd erupted again. Following the boy's example, they too picked up the spoils of the wedding and began pelting Ishmael.

"Break the curse!" shouted the hag, throwing a soft tomato.

"Yes, break the curse! Ishmael must go," cried the old man, bending to pick up some slop.

"Leave now," bellowed the merchant. He pointed a strong arm at Ishmael, blocking his path.

Ishmael's heart raced. He realized he was in grave danger. Running, he stooped and dodged the rubbish. A jagged piece of bone caught his shin, and he screamed in pain, the blood trickling on his clothes. Something hard hit his neck, smarting.

"You'll see," he cried. "You'll all see." He turned to his cronies. "Men, if you have the guts, you'll join me. Tonight!" Then he fled, humiliation burning within him as his legs pounded.

That night, Ishmael waited hidden in the dark shadows of his home. He lit no candles in case the townspeople found him. His clothes were torn and stained, the stench of the rotten food filling his nostrils. Tears streaked his face when he remembered the sweet and chubby face of his daughter Ali.

"I had no idea how much I loved that little girl," he whispered aloud, remembering her bright eyes and soft curls. "I was too busy making gold to realize it." Loneliness ripped his soul. Remembering Ali's bruised little body when she lay dying of the plague, he was overcome with remorse. "I'm sorry I didn't help when you were so sick. I was just too scared. And now I've lost both of you."

Confusion filled him when he thought of Adiva. "Oh, Adiva. Don't you know that I was only doing all this to give you more?" But he knew in his heart that he was lying to himself. He had done it all out of pride.

Ishmael lay crumpled for what seemed hours until the sound of crunching steps outside startled him. He leapt up, snatched a stick, and crept to the door. He flung the door open with a loud creaking sound, but his grip loosened when he recognized his own men.

"You've come after all," he said, wiping his sweaty brow.

"We're hungry," one of the men mumbled.

"Adiva's gone," he said, his voice cracking for only a second, "but I'll cook you something."

With that, Ishmael fed the men, explaining his observations about the unicorns to surprised ears while they ate. He enjoyed the men's attention and was soon plotting the capture of more unicorns.

Who needs Adiva when there are more unicorns to capture?

With the appearance of his men, Ishmael had lost all remorse.

Chapter Twenty-Two

The Final Battle

For days, the unicorns huddled together, hidden in the depths of the sombre gray forest, waiting for the backlash of Zackary's foolhardiness. Zackary sulked outside of the group, gazing to the mountains beyond. Azaria felt sorry for his cousin, but knew he had to be firm.

Several days later, they came.

Azaria saw them from afar as Ishmael and his cronies moved steadily toward the unicorns' hiding place. "Camouflage!" he cried.

Within a few seconds, the unicorns blended into the landscape, frozen and scarcely breathing.

The humans drew up smirking.

"Stinks like live unicorn," said Ishmael, scrunching up his nose like a rat. He turned to his cronies, sneering. "Must be one around here somewhere. Hmmm...now let's see."

He raised his bow and pulled an arrow from his quill. Drawing the arrow back, he aimed at a rock. It whistled through the air and struck its mark with a smack. A wild-eyed unicorn burst forth from what had been the boulder. It squealed and galloped away. His heart pounding, Azaria dared not breathe.

With a loud snap, Ishmael released another arrow into the large stump of a fallen tree. Angry as a wildcat, Polaris sprang from the tree stump, an arrow thrust in his side.

"Fly!" the Great Stallion roared.

Unicorns erupted from the trees, rocks, and bushes after their leader. They rode the wind, their neighs piercing the air until they arrived a safe distance away. There they stopped, gasping for breath, their faces filled with terror. Azaria did a quick count—there were five casualties.

"Quickly," ordered Aurora. "We must heal the wounded."

The mares moved in and tended to the injuries.

"Ishmael's figured it all out," said Azaria, puffing. "He knows we're not spirits, and now he's convinced the others."

Polaris shook, his eyes rolled back. "So then all we can do is flee."

"I'm afraid so." Azaria nodded. "When we see them coming, we mustn't camouflage anymore. So long as they can smell us, they can find us. We have to escape first, and then blend later when we're outside of their vision."

"Then so be it," said Polaris, struggling to catch his breath.

He's too old for this. I have to protect him. He's not like the father I've always known.

The chase continued, the humans in hot pursuit, the unicorns barely escaping. Three more mares were hit. Taking just enough time to heal their wounds, they fled once again.

"How long can this go on?" asked Aurora after several hours. "The mares carrying foals need rest."

"I don't know," said Polaris, his voice strained.

"Father, we can lure the humans from the rest of the herd if we outsmart them," said Azaria. "If we distract them with a few of the young stallions, then the mares can slip away."

"I agree," said Aurora, drawing up close to her mate. "We really need to get them to safety or we'll lose the foals."

"Let's do it."

Aurora led the mares away, while Azaria gathered up his buddies and explained the plan.

Zackary smiled. "That's my kind of fun. Thanks for including me," he said, looking down at the ground.

"You're welcome," said Azaria. "And Zackary...we all make mistakes, you know. Yours just happened to be a very dangerous one. It's all forgotten."

Zackary smiled sheepishly. "Thanks," he mumbled.

The young unicorns lay in wait, camouflaged, until they heard the clip-clopping of the horses' hooves against the rough stones.

"Now!" commanded Azaria, dropping his camouflage and whinnying in a mocking way. Ishmael drew his weapon.

"Over here, buddy," called Zackary, neighing on Ishmael's left.

"What?" said Ishmael, looking at Zackary, and then back to Azaria. He released the arrow in Azaria's direction, but the unicorn was already gone. Turning back, Ishmael found Zackary missing too. Then Gaelan appeared in the forefront, Azaria opposite him. Bewildered, Ishmael aimed and missed again.

"What the...What's going on here?" he grumbled.

"I don't know, boss," said one of the men. "They just keep disappearing."

"Keep chasing them," commanded Ishmael.

The chase continued for several hours until the sun sank low in the sky, and the humans pulled up their horses.

"Let's call it day. "We'll try again tomorrow when the light's better," Azaria heard Ishmael say. The men laid out their camp and settled for the night.

Azaria turned to his fellow stallions. "Let's go on a little further ahead. We can take turns sleeping. But one of us must keep watch at all times." He turned to Zackary. "Zackary, can you be the first?"

"Be glad to." Zackary stood at attention.

"Then you must stay hidden close to the trail while we sleep among the trees."

"Yes, sir," Zackary said, a smile touching his lips.

The young stallions kept vigil through the night, changing sentries every few hours. Azaria was the last to keep watch at dawn when the tell-tale sign of smoke curling high into the sky announced the humans were awake.

"All up, guys," he commanded. "They'll soon be here."

Despite their grogginess, the unicorns came to life, the confused scramble of their hooves beating the ground. Azaria waited and listened until he saw the sign he was looking for—the mushroom-shaped cloud.

"You see that big puff of smoke? It means they're putting out the fire. It's time."

The unicorns placed themselves strategically and waited.

The plodding sound of the horse's hooves echoing in the mountains reached them long before the humans did. Azaria gave the signal and the game began again—the crisscrossing and zigzagging.

"Hey buddy, over here!" Zackary mocked.

"No, over here," called Nathaniel, laughing.

Ishmael's arrow flew, barely grazing Zackary.

Gaelan dove past Zackary, galloping to his left. "*That* I don't like. Try *me*," he called.

"No, me," hooted Azaria.

Again, the arrow whizzed through the air, this time striking Gaelan full in the chest.

"Fly!" Azaria cried. "They're onto us."

The group retreated full force up the pathway until they were a safe distance from the humans. They only paused long enough to heal Gaelan.

"Father," said Azaria, "we need to get as far away from this madman as possible. He's too smart."

"I'm afraid you're right," Polaris agreed. "But we have to protect the mares too."

The clatter of hooves grew louder. Again, the unicorns escaped, but the humans kept advancing.

"Father, we're getting too close to the mares. We need to do something quick," Azaria warned.

Polaris looked beaten. "I know. Go ahead and warn the mares. I'll stay behind. If they see someone who seems like an easy target, they'll leave the rest alone."

"But that means you could be killed." Azaria gulped, fighting back the shock of what his sire was proposing. "You can't go alone."

"Azaria, I'm old now. I've been leader for a long time. The herd doesn't need me anymore. They need someone strong and young like you. I want you to follow in my footsteps and keep this herd alive."

"Does that mean...?" Azaria stared incredulously at his sire.

"Yes it does. I knew it would be you when you were very young. You showed signs. Remember the time I took you up the mountain top?"

Azaria nodded.

"I said you *might* be chief someday, but I knew even then it would be you."

"But Father, I need you. We all do. You can't just..."

"It's the only way, my son."

"No..."

"Things have changed. Now stand at attention," Polaris commanded.

Azaria stood straight and tall, knowing it was the most important moment of his life.

Polaris bowed his head and placed his horn over Azaria's shoulder. "I name you the Great Stallion of the herd," he said in the formal voice he used with Saul so long ago.

"Even over Zeus?" Azaria's eyes widened.

Polaris nodded.

"But Father…"

"Now go and take your place before there are no stallions left to lead."

Azaria stared at his father in shock, and then trotted to where the young stallions awaited him. "Fly!" he ordered, rearing high into the air. "To the mares. They've rested and we must move them out!"

"But..." argued the stallions, "the humans will only follow us."

"Polaris' orders," he shouted.

Azaria flew, his head forward to hide the tears. His anger and rage spurred him onward at greater speed. Flying to the top of the ridge, he turned one last time and looked down to the scene below as the others soared by. He saw the arrow whiz through the air and strike Polaris in the heart when he reared to fight off the humans. He saw the noble leader's stunned look as his muscles suddenly collapsed, and he crumpled to the ground. Azaria's heart broke. His eyes stung. But he wasn't ready for what came next. Before Polaris breathed his last breath, Ishmael sawed off his horn, brandishing it to the victory cries of his cronies. Choked, Azaria turned away, his mind made up.

He flew, enraged, breaking through brambles and brush, his coat full of cuts and bruises. He galloped through mud, and slipped and fell on his side. Rising again, he realized he had sprained his hock. Testing the ankle a few times, he grimaced with pain.

I have to find the herd quickly or I'm doomed.

He broke into a canter, taking the weight off the wounded leg.

The moon had risen, creating long eerie shadows by the time Azaria arrived in the canyon where the herd hid. He stumbled, exhausted, into the group, and was immediately surrounded by concerned unicorns, all mumbling and whinnying at once.

"Leave him be," ordered Aurora, "until he's been looked after. There'll be time for questions later."

Aurora tended to his flesh wounds, and Gaelan manipulated his hock. Azaria flinched until the heat of Galen's horn relieved the injury. Cassi and

115

Jemmi led him to the cool water of the lake where they washed away the mud and blood.

After he rested, he turned to Aurora. "Father is dead, Mother," he said, his voice thick with emotion.

Aurora broke into sobs and pressed her face against his.

"He died for all of us," Azaria continued, standing tall, his muscles rippling in the moonlight. "He gave up his life so we could live on. He said it was what was meant to be." Azaria told of his father's bravery as he went to meet the humans, and how they had murdered, and desecrated his body. The unicorns lamented, their mournful cries echoing in the mountains.

"Silence!" shouted Azaria with authority. "Do you want them to find us?"

The unicorns stared in shock at his fierce order.

"Our lives have changed forever. We cannot return. We must vow never to venture near humans or their horses ever again. We must travel further and further into the woods where they can never find us. It's the only way."

The mares mumbled among themselves, eyes wide with fear and understanding.

"I am now your leader. Polaris named me before he died. We will begin this very night, our legacy—my legacy, the Legacy of Azaria. And that means that each and every one of you will pledge allegiance to me. As for our foals, as soon as they are able, we will train them in the arts of Darius."

The unicorns stood, stunned, awaiting his words. Not a sneeze or snort was heard.

Azaria continued, "And now as your new leader, I command you to bow your heads and take your vows."

Each unicorn lowered its head, pointing its horn toward Azaria.

"We will survive," he chanted, over and over.

"We will survive," the herd joined in, the power of the words overtaking them as they recited. It rose to a crescendo, and then died down.

Then one by one as they finished, they turned to follow Azaria, beginning their exodus, their heads held high.

Chapter Twenty-Three
The Destruction

Ishmael and his men burst into town like lightning bolts, shattering the quiet before a storm. He waved Polaris' horn high in the air like a victory sword, shouting as he rode. His men followed, whooping and hollering, their hair flying like savage banners.

A loud scream filled the air when they entered the town, the horses' hooves clattering against the stone street.

"He's killed another one!" a woman shrieked, snatching her baby as she hurried to escape the galloping horses.

"It's Ishmael. The curse!" cried an old man hoisting himself up with his walking stick.

The streets flooded with terrified townsfolk.

"He's done it again. Imprison him," someone cried out.

"Stone him!" An old lady spat the words like venom.

The cloth merchant shouted, "Yes, it's our only chance to break the curse. Stone him!"

"No!" cried Ishmael. "I tell you there are no spirits. They're alive. I have the great stallion's horn to prove it. Do you hear me? The great stallion! Do you know how much power there is in this horn?" He descended his foaming horse in one gallant swoop.

"Enough power to destroy us with his wrath. The town will be demolished!" shouted the merchant again. "Stone him!"

"Stone him, stone him, stone him," the people began chanting, their voices rising to frenzy.

"Ask my men. They're my witnesses," Ishmael shouted over the voices, still sure of himself. He turned to his cronies, and caught his breath. They had galloped away with *his* horses.

"Stone him, stone him, stone him!" the town folk's cries grew more urgent.

A grizzled man picked up the first rock and hurled it at Ishmael. It left an angry, red mark on his arm. An angry woman flung a sharp-ended stone that ripped his clothing. Ishmael cried in pain. Pebbles flew like hailstones and battered his face. Drops of blood oozed from his skin.

Ishmael ducked, protecting his skull. "I tell you there are no spirits. They're just unicorns! They're like horses!" he shrieked in agony.

The townsfolk continued to pelt him with stones until, from the din, arose a tiny but strong voice—the voice of a child.

"Stop!" she shouted. The noise quieted down a bit. "Stop!" she commanded again. The mob's noise faded as though the child's voice had cast a spell. The tiny girl pushed through the crowd, rose onto the damaged statue of Ishmael and cried, "Stop it, all of you. Don't kill him. He's my daddy!"

Her large soulful eyes challenged them, and her bottom lip trembled. Ishmael's heart broke in two as he stared back at those precious brown eyes.

"Ali!" he cried, his heart filled with love. "Ali, come here."

The child turned and glared at her father, defiant. Then she turned to the crowd.

"He's my daddy and I won't let you kill him. You want him dead because he killed the unicorns? Well, I can make him stop."

The townsfolk stood with bated breath, awaiting the bewitching child's next words.

Adiva pushed through the mob, and climbed beside her.

"Ali is right. Ishmael has committed no more than the crimes of pride and greed. He doesn't merit stoning for such a thing. We've had our differences, but you've all committed evil deeds too—every one of you. Remember the time of the fireball? You all stole, and some of you even killed. You're no better than him. I say we find an appropriate punishment, one that is long-lasting."

"But how will we know he won't murder another unicorn?" shouted the merchant, the fire in his eyes gone.

"Because *we'll* look after him and bring him food." She turned and faced Ishmael as though ordering him. "He'll stay in his dwelling and will never venture into town again."

"But the curse," wailed an old woman. "He has unleashed a curse on this town."

The mob broke into angry mumblings again.

Adiva hushed them. "So long as he remains far away, the curse won't touch us. And as for the horn, we'll lock it away until another plague hits our town. It'll then be put to good use so that the great stallion's death will have had meaning. It'll keep our people alive."

The crowd stood in silence.

"Are there any objections?" she demanded, her voice as powerful as a judge's.

Still the crowd remained quiet.

She frowned at the mob and waved an arm. "Then go now—all of you. There will be no stoning today."

The streets emptied slowly, revealing the piles of stone left behind.

Adiva and Ali walked Ishmael along the dusty road to his home, and cleaned his wounds.

"Adiva, please come back. I love you. And Ali—you're such a strong little girl. I just didn't think…" he begged.

Waving him away, Adiva said, "You've had many chances and now you must face what you've done alone."

"Please don't leave me. I don't want to be alone," he pleaded, his voice trembling as he spoke.

"You should have told us that before. It's too late now." She took Ali's hand, and the two turned and walked down the path to the town, the little girl turning back one last time to glance at her father.

That night, Ishmael sat alone in the darkness of his home, mulling over the day's events.

"No one understands me," he muttered to himself. "If they had just taken the time to listen, they might have understood what I was saying. The fools. They're all fools."

The scraping sound of a horse pawing the ground caught his attention.

"Ah, the horses. Must feed them."

When he stepped outside, he remembered his cronies had escaped with their mounts. His horse too had fled during the near-stoning. Yet he heard the distinct snort of an equine sneeze.

"What the..." he said as he turned searching for the source of the sounds.

Shimmering before his eyes, the form of a unicorn materialized, pawing the ground and drumming its hooves. In the mist he could see other unicorns too, moving restlessly behind it.

"I know you're not spirits!" He guffawed and flung a stone at them. The stone passed right through them. Picking up several other stones, he cast them at the unicorns, but again, the stones sailed through.

Ishmael turned his attention again to the first one when it dawned on him. "You're the mare, the one who saved my Ali," he said, his voice high and trembling.

The mare took two menacing steps forward and snorted. Ishmael backed up, his eyes wide with terror.

"I'm sorry. I'm sorry! I should have spared you, but all I could think of was the money."

The unicorn pawed again and moved a few steps closer. The other unicorns' neighs grew louder, their furious voices rumbling.

"No! Leave me be!" he cried.

Ishmael flew to the door and slammed it shut, sweat pouring from his body.

I must be seeing things. If I wait long enough, they'll go away. My God, have I gone mad?

He hid himself in the corner of his room, cowering under a blanket. The unicorns broke into their eerie but strange songs. They grew louder and louder until Ishmael could stand it no longer.

"Stop," he shouted, but they didn't.. "STOP! STOP!" He curled up, covering his ears. The unicorns sang their ghostly music until the early light of dawn faded them away. But it wasn't over. The unicorns returned the next night, and the next, and the next after that. Ishmael realized he would be haunted until his death for his crimes.

He grew weaker and more frightened every day. His dark hair and beard turned white and he grew very thin, often mumbling to himself as he struggled through each hour. Finally, one morning, when Ali and Adiva came to bring him food, they found him lying still in his bed, his eyes staring in horror, his chest still. Ishmael had died a haunted man.

Chapter Twenty-Four

Darius' Exodus

Darius groaned in his sleep. His muscles twitched, and his tail moved as images of desperate unicorns flooded his mind—unicorns fleeing for their very lives. And Polaris...Darius jerked awake, pushing himself up with his great huge forelegs.

"Polaris is dead," he whispered the shocking words aloud, his eyes staring out into the early dawn. A tear rolled down his immense cheek and his sides heaved. "Ah, Polaris."

Memories swept through his mind of the day when Polaris, Azaria, and Gaelan had found him while Maresa lay dying, and how they had taken him back to their valley and raised him. Polaris had been like a sire to him, and now he was gone.

"You saved my life but I wasn't there to save yours."

More giant tears slid down his cheeks and landed with a kerplop on the leaves below.

After what seemed a long time, the trickle in his eyes lessened and he heaved a huge sigh.

"But the unicorns are all right. They've escaped...with Azaria leading!" Wonder filled Darius when he spoke the last few words, and he smiled. "I knew you'd win the battle, Azaria. I just knew it." He shifted. "But what about me? Sooner or later, the humans will migrate to this valley and find me."

The dinosaur gazed at the horizon where the sun rose, and he breathed in the fresh scent of the succulent ferns and trees surrounding him. Looking around, memories of a lush valley abounding with dinosaurs filled his mind, of days when his playmates were giant reptiles, of Saul the leader, even the Rexus...until the fireball destroyed them all. Darius sighed again. He knew it was time to move on and that this would be the last sunrise he'd watch from his childhood home.

Waiting until nightfall, he began the long journey. He trudged along for several hours, enjoying the coolness of the air. Cicadas and frogs buzzed and croaked in rhythm, lending tranquility to the darkness. The fresh scent of flowers added a magic to his solitude. After a while, the sound of water bubbling lured him and he changed his course.

Finding the stream, he dipped in his head, taking in the sweet, cold, life-giving fluid. It cooled his legs and soothed his tongue. He drank for a long time, and then sat on his haunches to rest. He took in the beauty of the night, the magic of the forest regrown, the splendour of the mountains.

Ah, the mountains.

Following the slope with his eyes, he traced the incline until he reached the line where the trees thinned. He drew in a sharp breath.

It's them!

Tiny white dots pushed their way up the slope in the moonlight.

Darius nearly called out, but stopped.

I can't risk the humans hearing me.

He watched them climb higher and higher, his breath quickening. "Go, unicorns, go!" he said.

A sob caught in his throat. How he wished he could follow them to their new home—anything to avoid the life of solitude that lay before him.

Maybe I can.

Darius took a few steps forward, his giant feet shuffling on the stones of the riverbank, undecided, and then stopped and lowered his head. He knew it wasn't meant to be and that he had to continue on alone. It was his fate. Groaning, he blinked back tears and prepared to continue on his journey—until something caught his eye.

One of the white specks had stopped and turned. Darius watched, his heart racing, as one by one, the unicorns faced him.

They see me!

The dinosaur stared in wonderment. Though they were but mere white specks in the moonlight, he knew without a doubt they were pointing their horns at him as they did for only the Great Stallion and Mohala.

They're honouring me! Me! As though I were the Great Stallion!

His heart filled with elation.

It wasn't all for nothing!

He stood up to his full height and bowed his head in return. "Farewell, my friends," he whispered.

The white specks lingered as though reluctant to leave. Then their leader turned and led them up the steep slope.

About the Author

Suzanne de Montigny wrote her first unicorn story at the age of twelve. Several years later, she discovered it in an old box in the basement, thus reigniting her love affair with unicorns. A teacher for over twenty years in Vancouver, B.C., she learned she could spin a good tale that kept kids and teachers asking for more. *The Shadow of the Unicorn: The Legacy,* is her first novel.

Suzanne lives in Burnaby, B.C. with the three loves of her life—her husband and two boys.

* * * *

Did you enjoy Shadow of the Unicorn: The Legacy? If so, please help us spread the word about Suzanne de Montigny and MuseItUp Publishing. It's as easy as:

•Recommend the book to your family and friends
•Post a review
•Tweet and Facebook about it

Thank you
MuseItUp Publishing

MuseItUp Publishing
Where Muse authors entertain readers!
https://museituppublishing.com
Visit our website for more books for your reading pleasure.

You can also find us on Facebook:
http://www.facebook.com/MuseItUp
and on Twitter:
http://twitter.com/MusePublishing

CPSIA information can be obtained at www.ICGtesting.com
Printed in the USA
LVOW09s0732071114

412400LV00001B/8/P

9 781771 276153